REBELLION of THIEVES

★ "A satisfying and nuanced follow-up to this hit series. Readers will anxiously anticipate the next installment." —*School Library Journal*, starred review

"Suspenseful and action-packed. . . . Readers familiar with reality competition shows—and Hunger Games fans— will enjoy the Iron Teen element." —*The Horn Book*

"A fast-paced, futuristic adventure tale that will have readers feeling as though they've been on a physical and emotional roller coaster." —*Kirkus Reviews*

"Remains a perfect fit for reluctant readers in search of the next high-octane adventure series. . . . Fans of the first title will be eager for this one, only to devour it and crave the next." —*Booklist*

SHADOWS of SHERWOOD

★ "Thrilling. . . . This exciting page-turner will undoubtedly be a hit." —*School Library Journal*, starred review

"Call[s] to mind the Percy Jackson adventures and will inspire a new generation to connect with Robin Hood's timeless tale." —*Booklist*

"Set in the future and paced with one death-defying escape after another, Magoon's story doesn't end so much as pause." —*Publishers Weekly*

"The wily kid heroes and thrilling adventures will appeal to young readers." —*The Horn Book*

"A killer female Robin Hood series by the incredible Kekla Magoon." —*Bustle*

BOOKS BY KEKLA MAGOON

Shadows of Sherwood
Rebellion of Thieves
Reign of Outlaws

REBELLION of THIEVES

◅ A ▻
◅ROBYN HOODLUM▻
ADVENTURE

KEKLA MAGOON

BLOOMSBURY
NEW YORK LONDON OXFORD NEW DELHI SYDNEY

For Sarah, Christos, Paul, and Thomas

First published in the United States of America in October 2016
by Bloomsbury Children's Books
Paperback edition published in October 2017
www.bloomsbury.com

Bloomsbury is a registered trademark of Bloomsbury Publishing Plc

For information about permission to reproduce selections from this book, write to
Permissions, Bloomsbury Children's Books, 1385 Broadway, New York, New York 10018
Bloomsbury books may be purchased for business or promotional use. For information on
bulk purchases please contact Macmillan Corporate and Premium Sales Department at
specialmarkets@macmillan.com

The Library of Congress has cataloged the hardcover edition as follows:
Names: Magoon, Kekla.
Title: Rebellion of thieves / by Kekla Magoon.
Description: New York : Bloomsbury, [2016]. | Series: A Robyn Hoodlum adventure
Summary: Robyn Loxley plans to seize the opportunity to rescue her parents
from the governor's mansion by competing in the Iron Teen contest,
although success could bring unwanted attention from Crown.
Identifiers: LCCN 2016011496
ISBN 978-1-61963-655-2 (hardcover) • ISBN 978-1-61963-656-9 (e-book)
Subjects: | CYAC: Robbers and outlaws—Fiction. | Adventure and adventurers—Fiction.
| Government, Resistance to—Fiction. | Contests—Fiction. | Rescues—Fiction. | BISAC:
JUVENILE FICTION / Action & Adventure / General. | JUVENILE FICTION / Fairy Tales &
Folklore / Adaptations. | JUVENILE FICTION / Social Issues / Friendship.
Classification: LCC PZ7.M2739 Reb 2016 | DDC [Fic]—dc23
LC record available at https://lccn.loc.gov/2016011496

ISBN 978-1-68119-534-6 (paperback)

Book design by Amanda Bartlett and John Candell
Typeset by Newgen Knowledge Works (P) Ltd., Chennai, India
Printed and bound in the U.S.A. by Berryville Graphics Inc., Berryville, Virginia
2 4 6 8 10 9 7 5 3 1

All papers used by Bloomsbury Publishing, Inc., are natural, recyclable products
made from wood grown in well-managed forests. The manufacturing processes
conform to the environmental regulations of the country of origin.

≪CHAPTER ONE≫

Do Not Surface

The night was not dark enough to hide anything, least of all the girl slipping through the shadows along the edge of the abandoned church. She eased the loose piece of plywood back over the church's secret door and paused, listening for the sound of any passersby.

Beyond this quiet block, the sounds of traffic slushed through the air. It had rained earlier. The scent of the damp and the drip from the eaves and the glisten of cars under each streetlight told the story.

Robyn raised her sweatshirt hood to ward off the slight evening chill and to cover her hair. She wore an intricate, six-stranded braid, like the generations of Loxley women before her—a signature style.

It could have been any old evening. Most nights involved sneaking out to steal something. Food, supplies, whatever she and her friends needed to keep themselves alive another day.

Sleep, wake, steal. The pattern had continued, uninterrupted, for the past two months. Sometimes weeks felt like an eternity. Other times, they felt like the blink of an eye. After dark, she was never just Robyn. She became something more.

Stealing to get by wasn't enough anymore. Robyn and her friends were putting bigger plans into motion, acts that would definitely start to change things in Sherwood.

Whispers now echoed throughout Nott City about the girl known as Robyn Hoodlum. About the seeds of rebellion being sown in Sherwood County.

It could have been any old evening . . .

Except it wasn't.

Robyn should have realized that there was always going to be a day that changed everything. Everyone has such days from time to time; it's a fact of life.

Thing was, Robyn thought she'd already lived through hers. The Night of Shadows, they called it. The night Governor Ignomus Crown staged a coup that wiped out half of the elected officials in Nott City and appointed himself dictator and supreme ruler of the city. Robyn's parents had been among the "disappeared" Parliament members, the members of Crown's opposition party who had been secretly organizing to remove him from power.

Had Robyn survived the night by coincidence or

miracle or fate? It didn't matter. That night, her world had ended. What more could be done to her after that?

She didn't think this on the surface but deep down underneath. On the surface, she was cautious, like any good thief must be. On the surface, she looked both ways before she crossed the street, because she never knew what was coming. But way down inside, in the tiniest creases of her heart, curled a truth that would prove difficult to shake—a belief that the worst that could happen had already happened.

It made her bold. It made her daring. It made her hungry for something, anything, to make the ache of loneliness fade. It made her reckless, sometimes, though she always did her best to finish a job with stealth and style.

Simply stated, she had become an outlaw. An outlaw with little to nothing to lose. So as she slid out the boarded-up door of the wrecked church, thinking about what she had to steal tonight, it never occurred to Robyn that her life could be turned upside down again.

She moved restlessly into the cobbled streets. A slight, mysterious shiver ran up her spine. She tugged the cuffs of her supple black fingerless gloves, securing them over her hands. She thought she was alone, but she didn't trust the quiet. If anyone came, friend or foe, she needed her skin covered, lest they catch a glimpse of her Tag—the barcode ID tattooed on the back of her right hand. She needed to remain anonymous.

Her TexTer buzzed at her hip. She flipped it open.

Do not surface.

Robyn rolled her eyes, but the words caused her heart to trill at the same time. She turned the TexTer over in her palm. The message had not come from Key—the only person who was supposed to have this number.

It was the third anonymous message Robyn had received. And the mysterious texter's previous warnings had been spot-on.

The same someone, whoever it was, wanted Robyn to stay hidden tonight. But she had work to do, and it was past time to get on with it. Now she had to decide. Go or stay?

Robyn was restless tonight, like every night. Every minute of patience and planning challenged her impulsive nature. She wanted her parents back. Now. She didn't know where her father was, but she knew her mother was being held somewhere in the governor's mansion, in Castle District. Robyn was working out a plan to free her and the other leaders of the Crescent Rebellion being held in that dungeon.

If Robyn had her way, she and her friends would have stormed the mansion gates weeks ago. Of course, it would have been impractical. A failure for sure. They needed time, and information, in order to make a good plan.

Just this morning, they'd talked over it again.

"We have to wait," Key said. *"Until the time is right."*

"We've broken people out of jail before," Robyn said. *"You know as well as I do, you can't plan or predict everything."*

Laurel laughed. *"We can bust out of anything!"* She flexed her miniature bicep. Her arms were spaghetti-thin but wiry as steel.

"We need the rest of Merryan's map," Key insisted.

Merryan Crown, the governor's niece, had been using her unique inside access to gather information about security in the governor's mansion. Every few days, she returned with a batch of new intelligence— about the location of hallway cameras, rotation of guards—to help them determine the best route through the building.

"We'll have something better," Robyn said. *"Merryan herself to show us around."*

"But the plan . . . ," Key repeated. Robyn dropped her head into her hands.

Key and his plans. Desperate frustration sizzled through her body in a flood of heat, like steam. She felt completely alone, even while surrounded by this group of friends she had repeatedly risked her life for, day after day.

"Something will go wrong," Robyn said. "No matter how much we plan it out."

Laurel nodded. "We have to be able to think on our feet." She kicked her legs out like a tiny ninja, causing both of the others to laugh.

"You are a mess," Key said good-naturedly. "You think you can take out an MP like that?"

"Heck yeah," screeched Laurel. "They won't even see me coming. Hiiiiyah!"

And that was the end of the discussion. Everyone was laughing too hard. But even among friends, Robyn couldn't shake the underlying feeling of being on her own.

Tonight, she was actually alone. With the potential for at least some small action. If she waited for Key to come back, for sure he'd come up with some reason why she should wait.

The anonymous texter had cautioned against action, too. Should she believe him tonight?

Go or stay?

The task ahead of her was pretty straightforward. Go.

It had been several days since she'd taken any really meaningful action. She felt itchy, restless from waiting. Go.

The confession note, ready in her pocket, would be taped to some wall tonight, as evidence of her crime. It wouldn't be a serious confession, more of a taunt really, since the authorities had no idea who she was. Just that she was someone. A thief. Messing with them. *Go.*

Danger? More than usual? Maybe. The cryptic text offered her reason enough to stay—at least in anyone else's eyes, it would've—but Robyn wasn't that type of girl. The warning almost made her want it more.

≪CHAPTER TWO≻

Preparation

Thirty miles away, a short, slim man stood alone in a room, gazing calmly at his reflection in a full-length mirror. He smoothed his mustache with a finger and a thumb as he murmured to himself, rehearsing the speech he was about to deliver. Not the words, but the manner of their delivery. The words, he knew by heart.

He wasn't nervous. After all, he was the governor. No matter how he said it, the message would go out loud and clear, and the person it was meant for would shake in her boots. The rest of the citizens would accept his latest decree as guilelessly as they accepted all those that had come before.

He was rehearsing for fun. He pounded a closed fist in time with certain phrases, waved an open hand on others. The fist was better, stronger. Emphasis on the word *traitor*. Emphasis on the word *death*.

He loved oratory, what it could do to a crowd. Not to mention how it made him feel. To hear a pin drop in the public square anytime he took a breath, to hold them captive with something so intangible as speech, the way he spun the very air with carefully veiled thoughts. That special kick of glee when an audience of thousands surged to their feet as he concluded his remarks, willing—no, eager—to take part in their own destruction.

Soon enough they would know. Soon enough they would realize, but by then it would be too late. His power was close to absolute. It was only a matter of time before—

Knock, knock.

"Sir?"

Turning from the mirror, he glared at the back of the closed door. Schedules be damned. He was the governor, and he would speak when he was ready to speak. But he suppressed his annoyance, surveyed himself in the mirror for one last second, then strode across the tile and flung open the door, emerging from his private washroom into the gubernatorial office suite.

"Ready, sir?"

"Quite," he said, smiling calmly at the harried-looking media assistant who had come to fetch him.

"You're on in five." The lad had sweat rings around his armpits and was gnawing the end of his ink pen like it was dinner.

The governor nodded, confident.

That's what tonight was about. Making sure there would be not only a tomorrow but many days after that. Everything was going according to plan.

All throughout Nott City, television sets turned on automatically, flipped channels, and tuned in for an Urgent Gubernatorial Address to All Citizens. Little screens flickered with static, large ones cut every line of the image crisply, and no matter which sort they were looking at, the residents of Nott City clapped eyes on their televisions as their bellies flipped with excitement. Terror. Anticipation. Pride. Disgust. What they felt depended on who they were, and where they were, but they all felt something.

Car radios and music headsets tuned to the public service station. Movie theater screens flipped to black; concerts stalled as screens lowered over the performers. And in the poorer districts like Sherwood, where televisions and radios were few and far between, public address systems clicked on at every intersection, where speakers hung from light poles.

Those who were close enough to the governor's mansion left their screens unattended and flocked into the public square to watch the announcement live. They gazed up at the second-floor balcony, where soon the governor himself would emerge. Spotlights shone on his tiny elevated stage, and when his slight form appeared in the warm white glow, the crowds cheered and waved.

Governor Crown waved back, a practiced, dismissive floating of his hand through the air above the people as the cheers grew louder. They loved him.

"Friends," he declared, raising his hands. "My friends. You have proven yourself loyal, law-abiding, wonderful. I thank you for your devotion. I feel I can trust you now with a difficult piece of news."

Silence fell over the crowd.

"It has come to my attention," he intoned, "that we have a hoodlum in our midst, a traitor bent on creating disharmony in our beautiful city. She calls herself simply 'Robyn,' and I'm here tonight to ask for your help in bringing her to justice."

The crowd rustled, for this was a first.

"My door is always open to concerned citizens," Crown continued. "I've invited her to come forward, to air her grievances. She has not. Instead, she persists in breaking the law, and I can stand for this treason no longer.

"As of this moment, the girl who calls herself Robyn is a wanted fugitive, and the number one enemy of the state. Theft of government property is now an offense punishable by death. Information on this hoodlum's whereabouts will be rewarded. *Well* rewarded. I offer fifteen thousand Points for information leading to her capture."

It was a fortune . . . to some. Better than a month's salary for the average Sherwood worker. A year's, for the most down-and-out. Mere pocket change or the cost of a nice new outfit for Crown and the Castle District crowd closest to him.

"Thank you in advance," Crown concluded, "For doing what is expected of you. We will have order in Nott City again." And with that, the governor spun off into the darkness. The spotlights blinked and faded, and down in the square the wealthy people went about their business again, most of them not knowing or caring anything about that girl Robyn and her antics.

Perhaps the one person in all of Nott City who did not hear the live announcement was Robyn herself. While Governor Crown stood at the microphone, emphasizing words like *traitor* and *death*, and his voice echoed around the city, Robyn hummed along on her motorcycle, making for the construction warehouse near the city's western perimeter. Provisions had been made for this sort of eventuality, of course. The announcement would be replayed every hour on the hour for twenty-four hours to be sure that every citizen got the message loud and clear. Certainly it would also be the headline in the morning paper the following day.

None of that changed the fact that Robyn hadn't heard the announcement yet. So she pushed the text message warning out of her mind and followed through on the careful plan. She parked her bike in a copse of trees and paused to gather her courage and her bearings. Then she marched purposefully toward the waiting fence, thinking it would be business as usual.

≪CHAPTER THREE≫

Reward

Fresh Wanted posters went up that very hour, blinking onto public billboards and monitors all around the city. In the poorer sections of Sherwood, MPs wielding great, ripping spools of tape slapped paper posters up in shop windows, on bus shelters, beneath scaffolding.

The boy nicknamed Key stood speechless beneath a now-silent lamppost speaker, deep in the heart of Sherwood, watching them. When the MPs moved on to the next block, he peeled one poster off a Laundromat window and studied it. The likeness was poor, just like the last version, but this new sketch was more realistic. The fugitive girl looked more like a person and less like a shadow. The written details were exceedingly accurate: female, thin, athletic, five foot seven inches, black hair—last seen braided.

Key's mind churned overtime. The governor's words echoed in his thoughts. *Hoodlum. Traitor. Enemy of the State. Punishable by death.*

Most people would've seen this new development as a setback. Key understood the problem, but he also saw an opportunity for his friend and their goals. An unlocked door, a healthy challenge. A slice of victory. That was his strength, understanding the big picture.

This was a setback, maybe. Crown personally knew about Robyn Hoodlum. No more flying under the radar. The Sherwood MPs hadn't caught her, so the full force of Crown's law would come for her now.

Key grinned into the darkness. He looked to the sky, but there was no moon. Remnants of rainclouds still wisped overhead.

He'd been waiting for this day. For two months, their small band of outlaws had been pushing further and further, beyond just stealing to get by, taking tiny bits that would barely be noticed, only enough for themselves. Now they had a larger purpose—to galvanize the broken rebellion. Their work demanded the attention of everyone in Nott City, up to and including Governor Crown.

They had Crown's attention now. Key saw the opportunity unrolling in his mind like a spool of wire. Crown had just plucked Robyn from obscurity and handed her the chance to be heard all across the city. The chance to maybe, finally, excite the people into reclaiming what was rightfully theirs. Now was the perfect time to get the whole community on board with the Crescent Rebellion.

But they would still have to be careful. The massive Points reward offer was an unexpected twist. An unfortunate one, but Key wasn't overly worried. The people of Sherwood had protected Robyn thus far.

But Key also saw in Crown's announcement what he knew Robyn herself would see: a dare. A bald invitation to wreak as much havoc as possible before the chains came down and choked them.

Key raced toward Nottingham Cathedral. He had to get to Robyn before she did anything reckless.

Sheriff Marissa Mallet sat alone in her large, white-walled office, high in the District office building. She drummed her neat, perfectly lacquered fingernails against the screen that formed her desktop, thinking.

Behind the gentle tapping, Mallet quietly fumed. Crown's announcement had utterly blindsided her. She should have been told in advance. Sherwood was her turf. Capturing the hoodlum Robyn was her responsibility. Her MPs had put up Wanted posters. She had already instituted a reward and raised the girl's fugitive status to #1 Most Wanted.

Now Crown was undermining her authority over the issue. The promotion to deputy police commissioner was on the line. That job was supposed to be hers in a matter of months. Was Crown taking it away? Maybe it was already being stripped from her, promised to the sheriff of one of the neighboring counties.

Mallet pounded her fist on her desk. The surface, full of monitor screens, flickered.

She should've seen this coming.

The governor's chief of staff, Nick Shiffley, had been calling daily to inquire about progress in apprehending the hoodlum. Yesterday, the call had not come in. Mallet had not been so naive as to think that Shiffley's attention would so suddenly turn away from the situation.

The methods Mallet had employed to try to corner the teenage thief were failing. Robyn was making her look bad. This could not continue.

Mallet tapped her comm screen. The face of her lead MP appeared.

"Full district lockdown," she ordered. "No one in or out of Sherwood without direct authorization paperwork."

"Uh—"

"And make the inner district checkpoints active," Mallet barked. "Spot-check IDs and Tags for everyone."

The lead MP gulped audibly. "Uh. We . . . we are stretched a bit thin as it is," he stammered. It would take days to mobilize sufficient manpower to staff every checkpoint. Mallet didn't care.

"Detain and examine any citizens legally named Robyn, as well as any matching the hoodlum's physical description."

"Yes, Sheriff." Pause. "You think it's her legal name?"

"Call it a hunch," Mallet snapped. She punched a button, and the screen went dark.

It was more than a hunch, but Mallet couldn't afford to let anyone know her suspicions about the hoodlum's true identity. She needed the girl in hand first.

Mallet would see to it that Robyn couldn't walk down a street in Sherwood without meeting trouble.

Key slid between the plywood sheets, parting them just wide enough to fit through but not wide enough to trip their alarms.

"Robyn!" he shouted.

He listened for her footsteps as he moved along the wall to check the intruder alert panels. Scarlet and Robyn had set up an elaborate system of trip wires and cameras to notify them of unauthorized entry. All looked good.

"Robyn!" he tried again. "Can you even believe this?"

"I sure can't," came a gruff voice from the rear pew.

Key flinched in surprise. The shadows of the cathedral hid the man's face. "You're here."

"'Gainst my will," the voice grumbled. "Nessa's got a way of talking people into things. Liquid fire, that voice."

Key smiled. Nessa Croft's radio broadcast was one of the ways of drawing people into the rebellion. Some people, like Key himself, came willingly to the struggle. Scarlet was similar. Others, like Robyn, came more reluctantly. The rest, like Laurel, came folded in by association, or out of desperation. They needed all kinds.

Elements gather, all to fight. The moon lore spoke of a group coming together from disparate places, with energy fueled by the natural elements: earth, air, water, and fire.

"Nessa's downstairs?" Key approached the older man, who nodded.

"Should be about done broadcasting. She'll be along in a minute." His lanky frame sprawled across the once-plush green felted pew pad. "Decent digs you got here," he commented.

"It gets the job done," Key agreed.

"Speaking of fire . . ."

"Did Robyn see you?"

"Naw," the older man said. "Nessa walked around. Ain't nobody here but you, me, and the church mice."

Key sighed. "She went anyway, I assume. Never listens to anything I say."

A rare laugh echoed in the sanctuary, scratchy and rich. "That girl ain't born to listen. She's born to lead. Don't you forget it."

"I don't know." Key plopped down in a pew. "Most of the time I think you're wrong about her. She doesn't want anything to do with the Crescendo."

"When she's ready, you'll know it."

"Will she ever be ready?"

The older man sighed. "You help her, you hear? Don't worry about the other. Nessa and I gonna rally the troops."

"I just want what's best for the rebellion."

"Hmmmph."

"Honestly."

"Then you gotta bide your time."

The wiring on the construction lot fence was pitifully thin. Barely as sturdy as a regular chain link. Robyn removed a set of wire clippers from her pack. They looked like a cross between a toolbox wrench and a very large pair of scissors. Placing one hand on each handle, Robyn clipped her way through a column of fence rings until the space was tall enough. She bent the fence aside and squeezed through. Easy peasy.

Two high-walled warehouses for storage, one tiny staff building for hand tools and lockers, one garage for equipment repair. Stamped on the door of each one, the logo of the Nott City Department of Construction. Beyond them were rows of parked construction vehicles: bulldozers, steamrollers, dump trucks, cranes, little machines that dig.

Robyn was after something much smaller. She reached into her jeans' front pocket for the gum wrapper on which Key had drawn the map of the second warehouse. Rows of shelves outlined in Key's neat handwriting, with a star to mark the right spots. He was a good artist, and an even better advance man. If he drew it, that was how it looked.

This time, he'd drawn something pretty straightforward. If all went well, she'd be in and out in a matter of minutes.

She glanced back at the buildings. The garage was dark. The warehouses had no windows, but lights shone from another building. The night-shift staff was already on-site.

All things considered, the place was quiet enough. She darted to the door of the second warehouse.

At that point, her task was half done. Now, she just had to get the stuff and get out.

She pulled a small black pouch out of her pocket. She hesitated, but only for part of a second. What she was about to do was technically wrong. Illegal. But there was something else she cared about more than the law.

So she extracted her lock-picking tools from their pouch and bent over the doorknob. Thirteen seconds later, she slipped through the door. Two seconds after that, she was striding among the shelves and boxes, following Key's careful directions, turn by turn, with a tiny beam of light guiding her way.

She didn't hear the alarm, because it was silent.

≺CHAPTER FOUR≻

Shelves

The alarm was silent in the warehouse, but when Robyn breached the door, little bells began ringing in three separate rooms in three separate buildings. Two of those rooms were very close by. One was rather far away.

The alarm rang in the foreman's trailer across the lot. He was standing in the yard and heard the ringing through the trailer walls.

The alarm also rang inside the small staff building, where a night crew of eleven construction workers sat drinking coffee and telling good-natured jokes about their wives and children. The bell sounded and they lowered their coffee mugs slowly. They were not security guards. They were strong guys wearing hardhats and steel-toed boots, but they were trained to drive backhoes and pour concrete, not secure a perimeter.

It wasn't the kind of place anyone really expected

to ever be broken into. They kept locks on the doors because the equipment was valuable, but they didn't take the locks very seriously.

The foreman burst through the door, a little out of breath. He began pointing at pairs of men and issuing orders. The crew scurried off to do his bidding.

The alarm also rang in a third room, way on the other side of town, nestled deep in an office building, at the end of a dead-end corridor, behind a thick steel door labeled Nott City Security Co. One guy heard it: a security tech working the night shift, alone. He wheeled his chair along a console full of buttons and TV monitors until he found the one he needed. His fingers tapped a keyboard, swiftly logging the location and exact time of the breach. Then he reached for the phone and made three calls, one after the other.

First he called the construction site to confirm the breach. The foreman he spoke to clearly had insufficient training to deal with an intruder situation, so the tech guy hung up quickly and called the MPs.

The third call didn't have far to go. It zipped along the phone lines of the tech guy's very own office building. It started in his secure station in the basement, and ended with a ringing phone thirty floors above him. The pleasant female voice that answered said, "Governor Crown's office. How may I help you?"

》》⟶

Robyn found the correct shelves with no trouble at all. She stuck her penlight in her mouth, then knelt and pulled her backpack around to her front. She opened the zipper and loaded it up with reflective orange safety vests, emergency roadside flares, and a couple of helmets. NCDoC standard.

Then she ran deeper into the warehouse, in search of their stash of orange traffic cones. She found them near the far back corner. She wrestled with the stacks for a while, testing the cones' weight. She found she could carry and maneuver a stack of ten easily enough. Ten ought to be plenty.

Like taking candy from a baby, Robyn thought. She offered the cones a gentle smile. She sheathed the stack in a big black plastic bag, to cover their bright color and reflective stripes. Then she hefted her selections and flipped them over, hugging them to her chest like a giant ice-cream treat.

Her TexTer vibrated in her inside jacket pocket. Only two people had this number. One of them had already sent a message tonight, and one of them was Key, who would never text her during a heist, unless . . .

Robyn dug out the device and snapped it open. Anonymous.

You triggered an alarm. Cut and run.

Robyn waited a beat, in case there was more. Then she tucked it away.

Out of sight, the warehouse door lurched open.

Trouble.

Robyn's heart pounded. She listened to the sound of boots on the packed dirt floor. Two men, maybe three. Four if she was really unlucky. Then she heard a loud buzz and hum. Instantly, the fluorescent lights far overhead snapped on one by one, like a line of dominoes.

Robyn was no stranger to trouble, nor it to her. They'd come pretty close to being good friends. Frenemies, her crew might say.

Robyn tightened the straps securing her backpack. Still hugging the cones, she crept to the end of the row, peeking around the boxes. No one in sight. Yet.

She sighed. Right on the heels of trouble came decision time. Take the cones, or leave them? The anonymous text had said cut and run. Did he know something she didn't?

No time to dwell. Robyn opted to take the cones. She could always drop them later, but if she left them now, there'd be no going back.

She tiptoed away from the searching men. Key's map showed other exits: two people-size doors cut into the long walls near each end, and two truck-size garage doors that took up the short ends of the building.

Robyn hustled through the maze of shelves and boxes toward the nearest person-size door. She caught sight of the exit, a door with a pebbled-glass window near the top, but didn't run for it. Call it caution, or hesitation, or intuition. Instead of running, she stopped.

Shadows crossed the glass, and the door burst open. Robyn froze, concealed by metal shelving that held stacks of heavy-looking cloth bags. Full of cement powder, maybe. Robyn watched through the gaps in the bags as two more men entered.

She was out of time. And out of places to hide.

Robyn hugged the orange plastic cones. Plan B: Drop and run?

No. That meant giving up on the mission, and if she was going down today, she wanted to go down swinging. So she hugged the orange cones, stood quiet, and waited.

The searchers were big muscular guys, in heavy boots. Any one of them could probably have deadlifted her plus the backpack plus the cones and chucked them all over the fence without breaking a sweat. But she was lightweight, long-legged, and fast. If she'd been a regular teenage girl, not an outlaw, she might have gone out for track or cross-country or soccer or something like that.

The two guys tromped down the neighboring aisle, their heads swinging back and forth atop their meaty necks.

Trouble.

The big, bad kind. The kind she had danced her way

around for the better part of a year. The kind that would eventually catch up to her.

She held no illusions that she could stay out of trouble forever. But she didn't drop the cones. She prepared to run.

Because her streak didn't have to end today.

≪CHAPTER FIVE≫

Luck

One thing Robyn had learned for certain in her twelve years on earth was that luck made a big difference a whole lot of the time. Sometimes luck fell on her side, and sometimes it fell against her.

The workers who busted into the warehouse had never been taught how to search an enclosed area. Instead of splitting up to cover more territory like trained MPs would have, they stayed together. So Robyn got lucky. As they moved toward the center of the warehouse, she shadowed them, moving the other way, keeping shelves between herself and them at all times.

She planned to circle all the way around to the door they had just come in, but it turned out she didn't have to go that far. The truck door at the end of the warehouse was jacked open, frozen about a foot off the ground.

Maybe it had a faulty chain. Maybe someone had gotten lazy at the end of his shift. Either way, it wasn't fully closed, so Robyn caught her second lucky break. The gap was wide enough for her to lie on her stomach and slip through. She pulled the cones along right after her. She didn't worry about the scraping sound it made, because by that point, the men had started calling out to each other.

"Anything down at that end?"

"Nope. You?"

Robyn stood, grateful to have put one big problem behind her. She was outside the warehouse, and, so far, unseen. There were more problems to come.

Her gaze darted left, right, center. She had a choice to make. Which way to run?

She'd prefer to return to the slit in the fence, but if they'd found it by now, they might be expecting her. So she fought the desperate instinct to slink along the buildings, back the way she had come.

Straight in front of her was a thirty-yard expanse of gravel, followed by the rows of parked machines. In the darkness, they seemed huge and menacing and shadowy. They seemed to have teeth.

Decision time. Robyn hugged the cones and ran, full speed, straight across the gravel lot. She weaved among the steamrollers, diggers, cranes, and backhoes. She pressed her spine up against the treads of some tall vehicle and waited for the distant shout of alarm, recognition, a blurted "There she is!"

It didn't come. Something else happened.

A flash of light momentarily blinded Robyn. At the edges of the lot, portable floodlights snapped on. One was pointed straight at her face.

Robyn looked down at the gravel long enough for her pupils to contract. The floodlights weren't meant to be used in this location, so they pointed in various directions. They lit the yard, creating odd pools of bright and dim space.

She skidded toward a shadow but didn't quite make it. Movement flashed in her field of vision and she froze, then slunk slowly backward. Robyn glanced desperately around.

Cut and run.

It wasn't an option. The team's entire plan for tomorrow depended on her success tonight.

When in doubt, hide. Another little tidbit of useful advice from Key. Sometimes it struck Robyn as funny that she had become the poster child for outlaw-hood, when Key was the greater criminal mastermind. She was bold, reckless. He knew how to protect himself, how to hide. It never hurt to take a page from that book.

So Robyn held the cones with one arm—not so easy—and used the other hand to steady herself as she climbed the treads of the backhoe. She rested the garbage bag of cones on the driver's seat. Nondescript. Unnoticeable. Perfect. The backhoe's digging claw curled inward, maybe six feet off the ground. It was wide enough, but only just. Stretching herself over the thin void of air, Robyn slid her butt into the claw like a chair. She pulled in her arms and legs, ducked her head, and closed her eyes.

The security tech guy's call to the governor's office was transferred to the chief of staff. Nick Shiffley was the sort of guy who worked round the clock. Someone had to. He listened to the report, then hung up without a word.

"Crud," he said out loud to the otherwise empty office. Things had been quiet for a week, maybe more. No incidents. No issues. All quiet from the Sherwood front. Everything rolling along as usual—small people doing small jobs, keeping in line, causing no trouble. Just as the governor wanted.

A week without a peep from that traitorous hoodlum, Robyn. He had hoped the worst was over, that the governor's announcement would have put an end to it all. Her antics were exactly the sort of thing Shiffley didn't need mucking up the gears of life in his city.

Because he was alone in the room, Shiffley took a moment to wallow in his frustration. He laid his face in his cupped hands and screeched muffled curses against his skin. Then he stood up, smoothed his brown hair, and stormed into the next room. It was the governor's staff bullpen, a large office with twelve desks in it, some for administrative assistants, others for junior staff. Shiffley threw open his door, and it banged against the wall.

His underlings jerked to attention. Three thin young guys with loosened ties stooped over paperwork, each hoping the boss was about to leave so they, too, could go home and not look like slackers.

"Silent alarm going off in our construction lot," Shiffley snapped. He was an average-size man, but his presence easily dominated the room. "You"—he pointed to the one called Rossman—"follow the police band. I want fifteen-minute updates. You"—he pointed to the one called Clark—"monitor the WebNet for any chatter and kill it. You"—he pointed to the one called Jones—"get me coffee and order me a car. Five minutes ago."

"Is it possible it was a false alarm?" Rossman asked, turning the dials on his official radio.

"You're fired," Shiffley said.

Rossman froze. His mouth dropped into a stunned frown. Clark and Jones glanced at each other, visibly tamping down their hopefulness and reaching for sympathetic expressions. Clark's fingers curled to a stop over his keyboard. Jones's phone hand hovered in the air halfway between his cheek and the receiver cradle.

"Just kidding," Shiffley said. "Idiot."

"Yes, sir. Thank you, sir," Rossman stammered.

"Who has a better question for me?"

The three grunts sat in awkward silence. A hoarse voice from beyond them uttered, "What does she want with construction equipment?"

Shiffley flinched. "Get to work," he snapped, and the grunts hopped to it.

Shiffley turned toward the voice, that of his colleague and the governor's press secretary, Bill Pillsbury. The lanky bald man stood in the doorway with hands folded. "Pill, I didn't see you there."

Pillsbury smiled. "Yet here I am."

Shiffley returned the smile, a bit nervously, though he was more than a bit annoyed by his nervousness. He was in charge, after all. The governor was the governor, but he was the boss. Yet somehow Pill's presence always made him feel he was being . . . watched. Ridiculous.

"Needless to say, we'll need to keep this out of the news," Shiffley declared.

Pillsbury nodded. "Done and done."

"Thank you," Shiffley said. Creepy as he was, Pill knew how to do a job right.

"Sir," Clark interrupted. "Your car is ready and waiting downstairs."

"Very well." Shiffley cast one last glance over his staffers at work, then stormed out the door, tossing a reminder over his shoulder. "Updates. Every fifteen."

He didn't wait for confirmation from anyone. He had ordered it, so it would happen.

≪CHAPTER SIX≫

Hide and Seek

Robyn stayed curled in the claw of the backhoe for what felt like an eternity. It must have been an hour, at least. She waited until the sirens came, and receded. Until the footsteps prowling the lot ceased their crunching and the voices that accompanied them no longer swirled around her. Her butt fell asleep. Her knees ached from being drawn in tight. Her arms ached from holding them. Her mind drifted back and forth, from the present to the past to the future. She could see two of the three very clearly.

Her father's smile, her mother's arms, a feeling of home. The past.

The anonymous urgent message, her aching body, her aching heart. The present.

Nott City without Governor Crown. That was the future Robyn envisioned. Crown was evil. Not everyone could see it yet, but she could. She had. He had tipped his hand too hard and she had seen the cards. Two months ago, when Crown marched into power without regard for pesky little formalities like an election. Late one night, he quietly destroyed his opposition. He sent men to bust into their homes and take them out, one by one. And just like that, it was over.

At first, people were upset. But Crown was good on TV. He had a nice smile and people thought it was all going to be okay. The people who mattered, anyway. The ones with money and nice houses, who lived happy, carefree lives, going to work and going to school and coming home and always having enough of everything. Robyn remembered what that felt like. To be safe within the bubble of Castle District, with everything you ever wanted right at your fingertips. But she had a new life now. A life without, a life of longing. Her new people, the struggling people of neighborhoods like Sherwood, knew better than to trust Crown's tactics. They were the ones who paid when things got rough. The ones who, like her, knew it was time to take action.

Robyn waited until the commotion in the yard had ceased entirely. The floodlights dimmed and went off. The construction guys rolled out in some vehicle or another, off to start their night-shift work. She heard it all happen, then the air stilled, the way it does when you're alone.

Robyn held out as long as she could, for insurance, but the ache in her legs spurred her to shift position.

She unfolded her body and twisted out of the claw, lowering herself to the ground as quietly as possible. Then she looked around. It felt like no one was there, but Robyn wasn't taking any chances. She retrieved the cones from their hiding place and slung her backpack over her shoulders again. She crept through the maze of machines toward the fence, away from the main entrance.

It was not pitch-black. The ambient light from the rest of the city cast a gray wash over everything. The buildings loomed as great distant shadows. Two tiny lights were on over by the entry gate, possibly to light the way home for the workers when they returned.

Robyn slunk along the fence, headed back toward the slit she had used to climb in. No better way to get out, she figured. That had been her plan all along. She moved slowly, hoping she blended with the shadows. She pressed along the fence until she reached the spot where it bowed open.

She paused. In the middle of her quick escape, she'd forgotten the fun part. Robyn reached into her inner jacket pocket and extracted a small folded note. She unfolded the page and smoothed it. It was a half sheet of luscious cream-colored stationery lifted from the governor's personal office supply stash. Little added extras like that made her work all the more meaningful.

She couldn't go back to the warehouse. Instead she punched the note onto one of the clipped fence links.

The message read:

Dear Nott City Dept. of Construction,

I visited your warehouse this evening and helped myself to a few useful things. Please don't think of these items as "stolen." They have simply been borrowed by a concerned citizen.

Robyn Hoodlum

Robyn pushed the bag of cones through the fence, followed by the stuffed backpack. She squeezed through after it and tugged the straps over her shoulders again. She righted the stack of cones, then turned at the sound of something moving.

The floodlights flicked on, blinding her. Robyn grabbed up the cones and started to run but found herself face-to-face with a Nott City Military Police officer. She spun around, but there was another MP.

She was surrounded.

≪CHAPTER SEVEN≫

Training Exercise

Robyn raised the sack of cones higher, hoping to hide her face. The authorities still didn't know exactly who she was or have a clear image of what she looked like. She wanted to keep it that way as long as possible.

She put her back toward the fence as the two officers approached her from either side, guns drawn. She stood maybe two yards away from the fence, and they eased toward her.

Straight in front of her, the patch of withered grass stretched wide and open for maybe a dozen yards before blending into a copse of trees that arced along the property. Too far to make a mad dash for cover.

Robyn gazed longingly at the trees, where she'd hidden her motorcycle. The woods went all the way to the edge of Nott City and probably beyond, though it wasn't possible to go beyond. Not for her, anyway.

The sound of one officer's handgun cocking snapped Robyn's mind back to the problem at hand.

"Drop the bag. Put your hands in the air," the MP on her left said.

Her brain scrolled through desperate situation solutions.

Run. *And get shot? No, thanks.*

Hide. *Where?*

Deflect. *Worth a try.*

"Hands in the air!"

Robyn stayed in place without moving. "Well, you got me, boys," she said amiably. "Great work. You're bound to get a promotion for this. You've passed the training exercise with flying colors."

"This is no training exercise," the one on her right said.

"Sure it is. They never *tell* you it's a training exercise in advance. But you achieved your objective, so it's okay for me to tell you." Robyn glanced left and right. The cops kept their firepower pointed at her. It wasn't working. "Seriously, guys. Radio it in if you don't believe me."

"You're under arrest," Left Cop said. "I'm going to have to ask you again to drop the bag and raise your hands. Shiffley said—"

"I understand," Robyn said. "You want to carry it all the way through." She hoped her voice didn't betray her panic. Shiffley? Involving himself personally in routine police matters? The news shocked her.

She clucked her tongue. "You two. Top-notch. Really. You should be proud." Behind the cones, Robyn shook her head as if troubled. "Some of your brethren . . ." She sighed. "Let's just say there'll be a lot more training exercises to come."

She watched out of the corner of her eye as both MPs puffed up with the praise. Something was working. Time to give her story a real run for its money.

"So let's do it," she said. "Arrest me. But here's the thing. I just maneuvered my way through this fence here, and it wasn't as easy as it looked. I think I pulled a muscle in my back. I don't want to drop the bag. Government property and all. But I can't bend over to set it down."

"Oh," Left Cop said.

"Yeah. So, if one of you can hold this, while the other one arrests me, that would really be great."

Right Cop holstered his weapon. "I got it." He stepped toward her, just as she was hoping. He was a full-grown man, with a couple of inches and quite a few pounds on her. What she was about to do was foolhardy at best, but Robyn was nothing if not daring.

Putting all her weight behind the blow, she swung the butt end of the cones into Right Cop's chin, delivering a swift uppercut. Then she swung them around and smacked away Left Cop's gun arm. He had been lowering it, anyway, reaching for his cuffs.

The handgun clattered against the fence and fell away. Left Cop glanced at her, stunned. Right Cop toppled to the ground, unconscious. Robyn released the cones along the line of their momentum, which sent them tumbling to the ground at the base of the fence. She leaped forth under the same momentum and scooped up Left Cop's loose gun.

Robyn spun around and aimed it at his chest.

"Don't shoot," Left Cop pleaded.

Robyn sighed as if disappointed. "And you were doing so well," she said. "Next time, don't let any suspect get the drop on you. Even in a training exercise."

The gun felt heavy in her hand. Warm from the MP's grip and unpleasant to the touch. She hoped she looked like a pro holding it, but to be honest, it was a first for her. She wasn't about to pull the trigger. But one thing she knew about MPs is that they assume people with guns are likely to fire them.

"Kneel down," she told him. "Put your hands behind your head. And don't worry. You've still got higher marks than any of the others." She smiled gamely. He obeyed, looking chagrined.

One glance told her that Right Cop was down for the count. Robyn found herself doubly glad she hadn't left the cones behind. He lay on his back, and a line of blood trickled over his mouth. She couldn't tell if the hit had started a nosebleed or made him bite his tongue or what, but on her second glance, she didn't like the look of it.

"Down on your belly," she said.

Keeping an eye on Left Cop, as he sprawled beside the fence, she sidled toward the sack of cones and took a handful of the plastic bag, slinging it over her shoulder.

"I'm going to walk away now," she said quietly. "First thing you're going to want to do is check your buddy's airway over there. He's got a situation."

The officer lifted his head marginally, to look.

"Don't move," Robyn ordered. "Second thing you'll want to do is radio this in. Do me a favor. Tell Shiffley—"

More of the lot lights snapped on in a sudden blaze of glowing white heat.

"I radioed it in the second I saw you," Left Cop said, rising to all fours. "I'm a good officer, like you said."

"Don't move," Robyn repeated. Through the fence came the sound of footsteps. A line of MPs raced through the yard, toward them, guns drawn.

Robyn blinked. *Gotta go!*

So much for sweet talk. She turned and fled.

Men shouted at her back.

Shots rang out behind her.

Robyn hefted the sack of cones high to protect her head. When she hit the trees, she dropped the gun but never stopped running. There could be more of them. And they could come from anywhere. She'd wasted too much time trying to be clever. Trying to just walk away smooth.

Robyn charged through the trees toward her bike, hidden in the column of white birch trunks, easy to find even by the barest moonlight. She slapped the cone sack on the rear rack and secured it in place with the bungee cords that were ready and waiting. Then she hopped on, jammed on her helmet, kicked the bike forward off its stand, twisted the throttle, and shot forward out of the hiding spot. The sound would not go unnoticed.

She bent forward and drove as fast as she dared over the uneven ground, headed for the road. Sirens rose up around her, and as she cut toward the nearest city streets, she saw the MP jeeps circling the blocks, one after the other. But she couldn't slow down. She bumped over the curb, landing right between two rolling cruisers. The sirens whined more urgently.

She accelerated to road speed, zipping past the police. No way they didn't spot her. So she accelerated more.

Robyn rode hard, weaving through the wide streets, turning as often as was practical, trying to put a bit of a maze between her and the MPs. It was late and the streets were quiet. This part of Nott City, an area known as Block Six, was heavy on warehouses and storefronts for businesses that benefit from the use of warehouses, like hardware and paint stores, lumberyards, metal-work shops, auto-parts stores, and labor-union head-quarters. The kind of area where every building closes around sundown, if it was even open at all that day.

First things first. She had to ditch this ride. They'd be looking for a girl in black on a bike.

At the first chance, she shook into an alley. One she was familiar with and could find again. She skid-ded the bike in between two Dumpsters and parked it. She unlatched the sack of cones and crouched for a few minutes, waiting for any sirens to pass her by. They grew louder at first, and then began to fade. Tucked between the Dumpsters, out of view, she stripped off her black jacket and T-shirt. From the satchel on her bike, she pulled a baby-pink tank top and a dark-pink hooded car-digan. She slipped on a red beret to conceal her braid.

When all the wailing had faded into the distance, Robyn hopped up and strode out of the alley. She went straight to the curb, right to the edge of traffic, and stuck her arm up to hail a cab.

◄CHAPTER EIGHT►

Spitting Image

It took Robyn 197 seconds to catch a taxi. Well above the average cab-hailing time in Nott City, but not too bad under the circumstances. It was late, and even though she'd found her way to a main drag, it was still the edge of the warehouse district.

So, it took more than three full minutes before a cab curled around a distant corner onto the street where Robyn stood. She thrust her arm up urgently, and the yellow beast merged toward her as it churned along the blocks. It eased to a stop right next to her.

Robyn threw herself into the backseat.

"Sherwood," she murmured. "Anywhere west of Notting Boulevard."

"*West* of Notting?" the cabbie repeated. His tone held a statement and a question all rolled into one.

The statement: *I don't want to drive to that neighborhood.*

The question: *If I do agree to take you there, can you pay for the ride?*

Robyn tamped down frustration. She didn't have time for misplaced emotion, the kind that might get her thrown out of the cab, or worse, thrown into jail.

"Yes, sir. Please," she said. She dug in her jacket pocket for the slim wallet she carried specifically for moments like this one. She extracted a fifty-dollar bill and smacked it up against the bulletproof glass that separated her from the cabdriver.

"What am I supposed to do with that?" he snapped. He leaned toward the computer on the dash. "Give me your Tag number."

But she couldn't do that.

Robyn slid the fifty higher. "Oh, come on. It's a collector's item."

He studied her in the rearview mirror. Long enough to make her uncomfortable.

"Please," she said.

The cabbie slid open the tiny trapdoor and took the cash. The car rolled forward, smoothly and quickly, but not too quickly. The perfect speed, if Robyn did say so herself. Fifty dollars well spent.

They rode in silence for a while. The radio hummed pop-rock music at a low volume. Robyn kept her head low against the seat and pulled her hood up to hide her face again.

The cabbie lowered the radio. Glanced in the rearview mirror. Spoke furtively. "Are you her?"

"Who's that?" Robyn murmured.

"Yeah, never mind. I know you're her," he said. "You're Robyn."

"Robyn?" she asked, aiming for an innocent tone. True, she was the subject of many a rumor going around in Sherwood. The guy must live there himself.

"I've seen your Wanted posters. Spitting image."

Spitting image of a vague silhouette? Thanks, dude.

Robyn shifted in her seat, wondering if this guy was about to become a problem for her. Her wallet was still pretty cash-heavy. Her father had left her an envelope of old cash bills in case of emergency. Once Robyn figured out what they were, they'd started to come in handy.

Maybe another fifty would be enough to buy his silence. It always had been before. But this cabbie had an earnest, heroic vibe going, the kind that sometimes implied an I-can't-be-bought moral code. In Robyn's experience, those guys were interested in one of two things: helping her out, or turning her in. Either way, their eagerness often spelled trouble.

"Sir, I'm afraid you have me confused—"

"Is there an address?" The cabbie cut her off. "Someplace you want to go in Sherwood?"

Robyn breathed. "You can drop me in front of the old convenience store on Notting and Dozer." It was six blocks from the cathedral, but she couldn't very well get dropped off at her door. There was bound to be little activity in front of the closed shop at this late hour. Many shops and stores that used to thrive in Sherwood had gone out of business, thanks to Crown's new policies of consolidation.

The guy nodded. His gaze tennis-ball bounced between the rearview and the road ahead. He merged onto the highway, carrying her out of Block Six at a smooth, high speed.

The drive took more than twenty minutes, but the cab glided to a stop a dozen blocks too early.

"Checkpoint," the cabbie said. He made a swift smooth right to avoid the line of cars waiting to enter Sherwood County. "Dispatch says all Sherwood checkpoints are active. What do you want me to do?"

"I guess I'll get out here," Robyn said. She tried to speak calmly, concealing her alarm at the prospect of having to find a way home on foot. But she couldn't really see another option.

She started to open the cab door, when the tiny window in the cab's plastic wall creaked open. The cabbie shoved the fifty-dollar bill back through the slot. It dangled there, half-in, half-out, all green and tempting.

"Honored to drive you, miss."

Robyn pressed her gloved hand up against the thick pane. Waited until the cabbie did the same. Close as you could get to a handshake under the circumstances.

"That means more to me than the cash." Robyn grinned and got out of the car, leaving the fifty bucks hanging.

Robyn supposed there could come a day when she'd regret leaving that cash behind. No question, she could have used it. But her image mattered as much as her message. And actions spoke louder than words. Key had taught her that.

She hefted the cones by a fistful of bag and dragged them along the ground beside her. She'd have to go over the rooftops, probably. It could take the rest of the night to find a clear route back.

"Need a hand?"

The voice came out of the shadows of the alley.

Robyn startled. The sack of cones caught on a sidewalk crack and slipped out of her fingers, flopping to the ground.

"Oh, for—" Robyn muttered.

The girl in the shadows giggled. Her small shape darted forward and picked up the bag of cones. It was nearly as big as she was, but she was wiry from years of living on the street and hefted it easily.

"Some outlaw I am," Robyn said. "Armed guards, no problem. Laurel Dayle whispers and I wig out."

"Armed guards?" Laurel said, her eyes bugging wide. "Really?"

"Yeah, they almost got me," Robyn admitted, suddenly wishing she'd kept her self-deprecating humor to herself. "Good thing I'm fast."

They passed beneath the corner lamplight. Laurel's face turned wistful. "If I was with you, they'd never have seen you. I'm a good thief. No one ever knows it's me."

Robyn held back a smile. The ten-year-old was, in fact, the best pickpocket Robyn had ever seen. But swiping wallets and sweeping convenience-store shelves wasn't the same as going head-to-head with Crown's Nott City security. Laurel's eagerness to help the cause could get her in trouble if it went too far. Robyn wouldn't be able to live with that.

"I need you in Sherwood," Robyn reminded the girl. "You're my eyes and ears, remember?"

"Yeah. I see everything."

They walked along the mostly deserted street, Laurel leading the way.

"What were you doing here? It's late."

Laurel shrugged her thin shoulders. "Waiting for you."

"How'd you figure this was where I'd end up?"

"Key said."

Robyn shook her head. "Key's a smart guy."

Laurel nodded enthusiastically. "Oh yeah." Then she popped her head to the side so one of her ears cocked up. "Duck and cover!"

She dashed toward a recessed doorway. Robyn plunged in after her, having learned from experience never to doubt Laurel's sense of when to hide. They pressed themselves into the door's dark corners just as a Nott City MP cruiser rounded the block.

Robyn's face landed inches from a cheerful poster plastered to the door:

SHERWOOD IRON TEEN!

A contest of skill, athleticism, and courage
Ages 12–16
Winner receives 1,000 Points!
Sign up today!

Robyn felt an instant surge of nostalgia. She loved Iron Teen. She'd watched the contest every year back in Castle District for as long as she could remember, waiting for her chance to enter. It would've been this year, now that she was twelve.

The surge of nostalgia turned to anger. Yet another thing Crown had stolen.

The cop car eased on down the street past their hiding spot.

"I heard the tires," Laurel breathed, once the car had turned again at the end of the block.

The girl had some kind of sonic hearing, Robyn figured. It wasn't the first time Laurel had saved her from a potential hot mess. "Thanks. Where are we going?"

"I figured out the way," Laurel said. "That's what I've been doing."

Laurel led Robyn through the alleys and over the rooftops, back into Sherwood, toward the place they both called home.

≪CHAPTER NINE≫

Purpose

Robyn and Laurel climbed through the wreckage that used to be the Nottingham Cathedral's west wall. The "door" was a single piece of plywood they had loosened some nails out of, one of many similar wood slabs along the boarded-up wall. As soon as they slid through, it snapped back into place, smooth and in line with its brethren. Anyone walking past would see all the normal trappings of a condemned building.

Robyn checked the security, glancing quickly over the wire connections on her circuit board. Between her electronic tinkering skills and Scarlet's techie knowledge, they had established a pretty sweet setup. In the process, the two girls had moved from adversaries to almost . . . friends.

Robyn and Laurel picked their way through the rubble of stones and wood and metal until they reached the small staircase that led up to the suite of rooms on the side of the building. They climbed. In the upstairs hall, Laurel paused before reaching the office. "You good?" she said.

Robyn turned, taking the cones from the younger girl. "Yeah. Thanks."

"Anytime."

"You should stay in. Get some sleep," Robyn said.

Laurel's feet twitched on the tile. "Yeah, okay." She made for their bedroom doorway, but she didn't cross into it. She tapped her fingers on the partial wall and kept on moving, back to the stairwell. Back out into the night.

Robyn sighed. The girl was practically nocturnal. The streets weren't safe; there was all kinds of trouble a kid could get into, and Laurel didn't bat an eye about that kind of thing. But Robyn wasn't her mother. She didn't make rules, and she wasn't exactly a role model of how to avoid danger. So Robyn watched her go, pushed aside the twinge of worry, and continued down the hall.

She strolled into the office, lugging the cones and her backpack.

"I didn't know about the alarm," Key said, first thing. He sat in the desk chair with his feet up on the file cabinet.

Robyn shrugged. "Don't sweat it," she said. "I made it out all right, didn't I?" It hadn't been the easiest boost of her life, but it sure as heck hadn't been the hardest. Key ought to know that better than anyone.

"Still," he murmured, picking at the hem of his shirt. He was playing it cool, but Robyn could tell he felt pretty bad. "Tonight of all nights you didn't need an extra hassle."

"Come on, I got out fine," she said. "If whoever it is hadn't texted . . ."

Key closed his eyes. "Scarlet's looking into it." When the anonymous messages came in, they came to both of the team's TexTers.

"Okay." Robyn rolled him the stack of heavy cones. Their square bases turned awkwardly over the desk. Key absently patted them with his hand, as if welcoming them to their new home. Robyn slung the backpack up alongside them. It felt good to get the weight off. She extracted the vests and flares and laid them out. For a moment, she and Key gazed at each other across the desk.

It was a good haul, no question. Everything they needed for tomorrow. And the same stuff could even be useful for months to come. Maybe years.

Robyn sank into the threadbare sofa, fighting a wave of defeat. She hoped it wouldn't be years.

As if he could read her mind, Key said, "It's only going to get harder from here."

"You haven't even heard the real bad news yet. Shiffley was there tonight."

"Personally?" Key lifted his eyebrows. "You saw him?"

"No. I'm not sure he was really there, physically, but he was involved."

Key drummed two fingers against his lips and closed his eyes. His thinking pose. "Crown's not playing around with this new reward business."

"Reward?"

Key gazed at her, appraising her surprise. "Robyn?"

Robyn turned up her palm. "What reward?"

Key lowered his feet from the desk. "Are you kidding me? It's almost midnight."

"So?"

Key's face slowly split in a wide grin. "Oh, this is going to be fun. Come with me." He leaped out of the chair and grasped Robyn's wrist. "We don't have much time."

Key led Robyn down through the sanctuary and up the service ladder into the larger cupola at the far side of the building. Robyn came here infrequently; it was lower than her favorite tower, and afforded a bird's-eye view of only the nearby streets. Plus, its walls were intact, so all they could do was peer out the narrow window opening.

"What are we doing?" Robyn demanded.

Key was all smiles. "Where were you at nine?"

Robyn thought back. "Riding toward Block Six."

"Wearing your helmet?"

"Of course."

"And at ten?"

Robyn shrugged. "Um . . . hiding?" Curled in the claw of the backhoe. Her muscles still hadn't forgiven her.

"And at eleven?"

"Evasive maneuvers," she said. Dodging the cops? Running for her bike? Streaming through the streets? "Not like I was looking at my watch."

Key nodded. "Well, feast your ears on this."

Static crackled in the public loudspeakers. A mechanical voice droned. "Public announcement. Repeating, public announcement."

Then the air filled with Governor Crown's voice, smooth and cold as ice. This time, Robyn heard every word: *Hoodlum. Traitor. Enemy. Reward.* She stared into the gray sky, looking deep, as if she could somehow lay eyes on the speaker himself, reach out and touch the source of the threat against her person. If she could have reached him, she would have cut him down, that much she knew.

Key unfolded a Wanted poster from his pocket and showed it to her. The cabbie's words from earlier floated back to her. *"I've seen your Wanted posters. Spitting image."*

It was no longer a vague silhouette.

"We did it," Key said. "Public enemy number one, and not just in Sherwood. By tomorrow night, everyone in Nott City will know the name Robyn Hoodlum, and what it is you stand for." He continued, rambling excitedly about all the new possibilities. The power Crown had handed them unwittingly. "The people will rally behind you," Key said.

Robyn leaned against the dusty bricks and closed her eyes. It sounded so simple when Key laid it out. His words painted a picture that arced in front of them, all clean and meaningful, unlike Robyn's memories of tonight. The stabs of terror. The ache of curling tight so as not to be seen. The echo of bullets. The MPs' sweaty stench. Her own running footsteps, ragged breaths.

"This is only the beginning," Key exclaimed. "You're about to be a hero, in the eyes of every—"

"I know," she said, cutting off his monologue. "I get it."

Robyn breathed deeply of the cool night air. Pressed aside any hint of sadness, fear, regret. None of it mattered anymore.

The Crescent Rebellion was alive again. And she was supposed to be its leader.

The knowledge settled over her like a soft blanket woven of fate. It was always going to end up like this. It was always going to be bigger than her alone.

"I'm not just Robyn," she whispered. "I'm Robyn Hoodlum."

And everyone's counting on me.

≪CHAPTER TEN≫

The Moon Shrine

Robyn left Key in the tower and went down to the sanctuary alone. She climbed to the choir loft, smiling as she passed the mess of books and research materials left by Tucker Branch, the seminary student who had clued them in to the cathedral's secrets.

She skirted his desk and went to the locked door at the end of the loft.

Using the crescent-shaped half of her pendant as a key, Robyn let herself down into the moon shrine courtyard. She liked coming here at night, and she always preferred to come alone.

She climbed down the black stairs to the pebbled ground and approached the curtain. Six silvery strands, drifting slightly through the still air, as if on a breeze. The words crisscrossing each strand spelled out nonsense—until the strands were braided in the style of Robyn's hair.

She didn't bother to braid them tonight. The words of the curtain message were seared onto her memory at this point:

OFFSPRING OF DARKNESS, DAUGHTER OF LIGHT
GIFTING THE PEOPLE, BEACON IN THE NIGHT
EMERGE AFTER SHADOWS, HIDING HER FACE
HOPE OF THE ANCIENTS, DISCOVER HER PLACE
BREATH BLOOD BONE, ALL ELEMENTS UNITE
BLAZE FROM WITHIN, INSPIRE THEIR FIGHT
SUN FINDS HOME, IN ANCIENT RUNE
DEEP IN THE CRADLE, OF THE CRESCENT MOON

The curtain message promised Robyn was the one, the child and leader that the moon lore followers had been waiting for. The low pull in her belly that drew her toward this shrine, toward the curtain, seemed to agree. But the rest of Robyn didn't feel like the message could actually be meant for her.

Key wanted everything to happen at once. He could be methodical and patient in the moment, but he was in a big hurry to see a true rebellion take form. Robyn wasn't so sure any of them were ready to fight for real. Hiding in the shadows was easier. They could cause plenty of trouble and headaches for Sheriff Mallet and Governor Crown the way they were already doing.

Nott City seemed like a great place to live, if you came from Castle District. In Sherwood, though, Governor Crown's rules made it hard for people to make ends meet. Sheriff Mallet and the MPs enforced rules that kept food and other supplies restricted from the people. Everything was getting harder and harder for the working people in Sherwood. Crown wanted all the resources of Nott City for himself. He didn't care about anybody else.

The Crescent Rebellion was all about making things right for the people. It was all about opening the doors that Crown was determined to close. Robyn's parents had been prepared to lead this movement, but now Mom was in prison. And Dad—well, Robyn didn't know for sure if he was even alive.

Robyn pulled out the map Dad had left her. The cryptic old scribblings made sense to her now. She could see this shrine and the cathedral marked there. The tree house in Sherwood Forest where she, Laurel, and Key had lived for a while before they discovered the cathedral's secret.

Arrow symbols were drawn over the edges. The arrow design carried a hidden moon lore message, too: earth, air, water. Gathering the Elements had happened by accident. Each of Robyn's friends filled a piece.

Robyn had painted the walls with their circle:

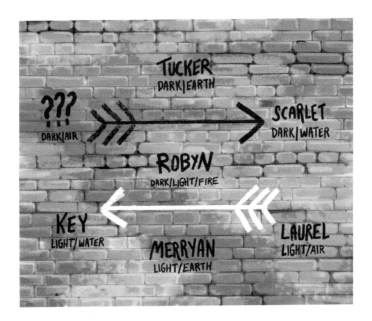

There was only one missing. A helper yet to be found. And at the center of it all: Robyn.

The fire. The last Element. The one who was supposed to ignite and fuel them all.

Robyn shivered in the dark midnight. Try as she might, she still couldn't see herself as the fire, as the daughter of shadows and light who could bridge the divides and pull everyone together.

She was only one girl.

≪CHAPTER ELEVEN≫

Plans, Interrupted

Robyn woke to the sounds of an argument. She rolled off her mattress, only to find herself alone in their shared sleeping room. Raised voices echoed off the broken walls.

"Don't be an idiot," Scarlet shouted. "We can't go through with it now."

"There's no better time," Key argued.

"They'll be gunning for us, big time," said a third voice. Tucker.

"We need the food," said Laurel, in her small but mighty tone.

"We need the exposure," Key added.

Robyn rushed down the hall and leaped over the brick rubble into the office. Key sat behind the desk, holding himself tall and presiding over the room. Tucker stood in one corner, Laurel sat cross-legged in another, while Scarlet half sat, half leaned against what was left of the opposite wall. Distance between them. The space seethed with tension.

"Hey, guys," Robyn said amiably. She set aside her annoyance that they hadn't woken her for the meeting. "Everybody ready for today?"

"Stupid," Scarlet muttered, from her perch on the half-caved wall.

"We can't lie low at a moment like this," Key insisted. "Especially since the plan to free the governor's mansion prisoners is ruined."

Robyn's pulse picked up. "Wait. What are you talking about?"

"The checkpoints," Scarlet blurted out. "There's no way we can get into Castle District now."

Key swept his hand over the surface of the desk. "All that planning, for nothing," he fumed.

Robyn's stomach knotted and sank like a stone. Mom. No chance to help her and the others stuck in prison there.

"No." She refused to accept it. "We're doing it. We'll figure something out."

"Not a chance," Scarlet said. "They'd catch us for sure."

"Can't you make us fake papers?" Robyn asked. Scarlet's techie skills had come in handy many times before.

"Are you kidding?" Scarlet said. "That's even harder than forging old cash money. There's special paper, special ink, government seals that they press the corner of the papers with. Plus, I've never even seen one in person, so I wouldn't actually know what to copy. I mean, theoretically, it's possible, but—"

"How long would it take?" Key asked.

Scarlet burst out with a laugh. "Weeks. Maybe months. And who knows, they might have changed the checkpoint protocol by then, anyway."

"We can't wait," Robyn said. They had already spent weeks working on the plan piece by piece with Merryan mapping the governor's mansion hallway by hallway, sketching guards, cameras, and other trouble spots. "We'll just have to find another way in."

"Maybe this is a bridge to cross later," Tucker suggested. He tapped his watch face. "We need to decide if we are going through with the truck plan. I vote no. Too risky."

"No," said Scarlet.

"Yes," said Key.

"Yes," said Laurel.

Stalemate. Four heads turned toward Robyn.

"We're going ahead with the plan for today, at least," Robyn said, putting as much certainty and authority into her voice as possible. Her words didn't sound much like a raging fire. Barely a spark.

"They're hunting you," Scarlet reminded her.

"All the more reason to act quickly," Robyn insisted.

Key nodded. "Robyn Hoodlum strikes again."

"And on the very day after the reward announcement," Laurel said.

"It'll be like a message to Mallet and Shiffley and Crown," Key said.

A new voice entered the room. "No one can keep Robyn, the hoodlum, down."

The group of outlaws turned their heads in unison. Merryan Crown, Governor Crown's niece, strolled into the office.

Robyn flinched in surprise. She hadn't heard the telltale clap of plywood, or the groan of the unoiled hinges from the old church door downstairs. If the intruder warning alerts had flashed at all, no one had noticed it in the midst of the heated discussion.

"Merryan, what are you doing here?" The words burst out rather more harshly than Robyn intended. As usual, Robyn's heart skipped with nervousness at the sight of the governor's niece. It was playing with fire a bit, letting Merryan know the location of the outlaws' secret hideout. But the news Merryan could bring from Castle District was very valuable.

"Oh, um, I came to see, that is, to make sure . . ." Merryan swallowed and shifted awkwardly. She pushed the toes of her delicate shoes together. "Are you okay?"

"Of course I'm okay," Robyn said. She crossed the room to meet Merryan at the door.

The short, curvy girl blushed, as was customary.

Merryan always seemed a bit nervous about things. She wasn't a natural outlaw, like Robyn or Laurel or Scarlet. Breaking the rules practically made her break out in hives, but underneath the thoughts about how she was "supposed" to act, Merryan had nerves of steel and could think quickly in a crisis. Plus, she had a whole adorable-innocent-rich-girl vibe about her that was really helpful in distracting the Military Police.

"What about Uncle Iggy's announcement?" Merryan whispered.

Scarlet snickered loudly over the nickname. *Uncle Iggy?* she mouthed to Key, who simply glowered. Laurel fought away a grin.

Robyn waved a hand. "Bah. They were already gunning for me before this. The reward just means we're getting to him."

Merryan nodded. If she had any qualms about the plot to pull one over on her uncle, it didn't show.

From behind the desk, Key cleared his throat. He did that kind of thing a lot, as if it were subtle or something. Obviously he wanted them to get on with the plan.

"Okay, back to business," Robyn said.

"We have to go," Key said. "The trucks will come through in less than an hour."

"Trucks?" Merryan's eyes widened. No doubt she was thinking of the time a few months ago when Robyn stole a truck full of food from one of Crown's storage compounds. Since then they'd been hitting supply warehouses around the city, in a random and hopefully unpredictable pattern.

Now, to be even less predictable, they were trying something else entirely.

The team quickly gathered the supplies that Robyn had appropriated the night before. Nothing could happen without those items.

"Yeah, trucks," Robyn said. "You in or out?"

Merryan's eyes widened again. Her round cheeks reddened. Her toes touched. "In."

Robyn smiled. "I'll explain on the way."

≪CHAPTER TWELVE≫

Under Construction

At the busy intersection of Notting and Sherwood Boulevards, Robyn's crew met up with their four volunteers.

"That's them," Tucker said. "On the diagonal corner."

Robyn could have guessed it. Their work boots and ragged T-shirts did not exactly help them fit into this higher-end neighborhood called Sherwood Heights. But they needed some big guys who looked like workers, and Tucker had delivered.

Tucker Branch: minister-in-training and volunteer coordinator for outlaws.

Tucker nodded to the guys as Robyn's crew crossed the street. The men followed the group along the block as Key led the way toward a more secluded intersection.

This narrower, residential street curved sharply. Robyn and her friends positioned themselves just in advance of the curve. They laid out cones to block incoming traffic on one lane.

Everyone worked swiftly and the setup took only a matter of minutes. *Teamwork*, Robyn mused. After growing up an only child, with few friends, she still struggled with the concept of operating in a group. It was so much easier to do things on your own. You just decided what you wanted to do and then went out and did it. Easy enough. But in a different way, having friends to help made things easier, too. It was more cumbersome getting started, but once the plan was in motion, many hands made light work.

Key talked softly, getting everyone organized and ready. Robyn handed out vests to the large men who had volunteered for the duty. Tucker wore one vest and stood in the street alongside the cones, positioned to stop traffic.

Robyn, Scarlet, Laurel, Key, and Merryan went around the curve to get out of sight. They crouched behind a set of brownstone stairs and waited.

The MPs were not messing around with security anymore. They had begun transporting food in long caravans, on secret routes that were revealed on the day of transport, and only to the lead driver. They thought they were clever, but the transport plan was far from perfect. The routes were kept on a computer. And they still employed ordinary staff drivers, not armed and trained MPs.

The drivers knew to look out for a group of kids. A small cluster of construction workers did not even raise a blip on the lead driver's radar.

The trucks rumbled toward the curve in one long line.

Tucker stepped into the street and held up his hands. He spun one finger as he approached the driver's side, asking for the window to be rolled down.

"Had a gas leak in the area," he informed the lead driver. As he spoke, he rested his hands on the window frame and stealthily pulled up the door-lock plug.

"Got a manhole open; we're fixing the problem. Hang on." He took a few steps back and looked around the corner, as if judging whether it was safe to pass. He motioned the truck to advance.

"Take the corner slowly, all right?" Tucker said.

"Thanks, man," said the driver, giving a little half wave.

As that guy turned the corner, Tucker held up his hands to stop the next truck. He gave the second driver the same story and stealthily unlocked the door.

As the first truck came around the corner, the other two grown-up volunteers, in their glowing orange vests, motioned once again for the truck to slow. When it did, they rushed the cab and pulled out the unsuspecting driver. When his foot came off the brake, the truck rolled forward. Key leaped into the cab and slammed on the brakes to stop it.

The volunteers were large, strong men, and they had no trouble subduing the driver and hustling him onto the sidewalk. Laurel and Merryan raced forward with rolls of duct tape and bound the driver's hands and feet together. A final strip over the mouth kept him from shouting out a warning.

The truck had an electronic keypad securing the rear cargo door. Scarlet went to work on it immediately. Robyn levered the door open an inch or two for easy access later.

When the door was loose, Robyn waved to Key, who drove the truck forward to wait for its friends. When the drivers turned, one by one, it never occurred to them that anything was wrong, because the full line of trucks still stretched out in front of them. One after the other, they fell into the hoodlums' trap.

They stacked the bound-and-gagged drivers out of sight behind the brownstone stairs.

The system became smooth. And fast. Less than sixty seconds per truck.

Teamwork, Robyn marveled.

≪CHAPTER THIRTEEN≫

Tension in Tent City

The next stage of the plan was to drive the trucks to different parts of the county. Each of the four adult men took one truck, plus Key, Tucker, and Robyn. Scarlet rode with Key, Merryan rode with Tucker, and Laurel rode with Robyn. They would separate the trucks, then throw open the cargo doors and let the people of Sherwood grab their fill.

Robyn held herself tall in the seat to try to appear old enough to have a driver's license. The truck's large steering wheel felt unwieldy at first, but it was not her first time driving a truck, and at least this time she could go at normal speed. They weren't being pursued by MPs. Yet.

She drove her truck to the outskirts of the county, near the old city fairgrounds. This was the most dangerous drop-off location. The MPs patrolled regularly along the edge of the woods and the perimeter of the fairgrounds. The massive empty lot had become a gathering place for people from Sherwood with nowhere else to go. A cardboard city.

Laurel raced ahead into the tent city and drew people out of their makeshift shelters to come and clear the truck.

The people came willingly, and fast. It was not the first truck Robyn had brought to their shores. The many whispered thank-yous bolstered her. This was what it was all about.

Two teens from T.C. came running up with a blanket stretched out between them. Robyn dumped sacks of potatoes into the makeshift hammock until it bowed under the weight. The boys chattered gleefully about the Iron Teen competition as they gathered the provisions. "I'm going to enter this year," said one. "It would be so amazing to see the governor's mansion."

"I've never even been to Castle District," said the other.

"Me either."

"If one of us wins, we can split the Points, and we'd both be rich!"

"Yeah!"

"Thanks, Robyn!" They laughed as they ran back toward T.C., each clutching two corners of the blanket.

Another young man from T.C. volunteered to drive and dump the truck someplace away from T.C. Robyn handed him the keys. His face shown with pride and determination as he slid into the cab. The truck rumbled out of sight. Robyn smiled. More and more people were stepping up to assume part of the risk for her heists. It both surprised her, and didn't, all at once.

Robyn and Laurel headed into T.C. on foot, looking for Chazz.

They found the older man lounging out in front of the makeshift shelter he called home, near the center of the tent compound. Laurel handed him a bunch of bananas and some cans of tuna from the truck. Chazz accepted the offering with a smirk.

"You don't know when to quit, eh, girlie?" He tossed the tail of his cigarette into the campfire burning steadily in the center of the circle of tents. It crackled and disappeared.

"Not till the job is done," Robyn said. She felt like a hypocrite, speaking with confidence when she wasn't sure of anything at the moment.

"They still gunning for you?" Chazz took a long drink from a paper-wrapped can, eyeing her over the rim all the while.

Robyn had a strong suspicion that Chazz knew exactly what was going on in Nott City at all times. He only wanted people to think he was down on his luck and slightly daffy. It kept the heat off him. Once upon a time, according to Tucker, he had been a leader of the Crescent Rebellion.

"Wouldn't have it any other way," Robyn said, grinning.

Chazz huffed. "Get on out of here, 'fore you draw more trouble our way."

Robyn glanced guiltily around. She had drawn trouble to T.C., sure enough. Just a few months prior, the MPs had burned the place to the ground because of her. The rebuilding was taking time, although it was a tent city, so they'd salvaged the sheet metal and whatever else they could from the ashes. People here were used to making the most of things. Chazz's hut consisted of fire-licked tarp fragments plastered together with duct tape and draped over a frame woven from tree branches.

"We got it," Laurel sang out, doing a little dance. "Trouble ain't met trouble till it crosses paths with us!"

Chazz rewarded her with a rare smile. The small girl was all breeze and charm. It was impossible not to like her.

"It's okay; we'll go," Robyn said. She wasn't even sure why she'd followed Laurel in here. The girl had wanted to deliver food to Chazz but really didn't need an escort.

Robyn found herself at the edge of the campfire circle, gazing down into the fire. In the daylight, the flames' glow appeared muted, but its warmth still radiated.

So much had happened since the day MPs stormed through. Robyn had been forced to claim her Hoodlum status, in front of everyone. She had failed that day. The tent city had burned.

But T.C. had been rebuilt. Not moved. Not destroyed. Recentered, in the spot that meant everything to the people here, on the edge of this tiny, perpetual blaze.

The fire that can never go out.

≪CHAPTER FOURTEEN≫

A Possible Solution

"Look, I don't care what Key and Scarlet think," Robyn told Laurel as they headed back to the cathedral to meet up with the others. "I still have to find a way to get into the governor's mansion."

"I know," Laurel said.

"You do?" Robyn smiled. At least one person might be on her side.

Laurel ducked her head. "If I had a mom, I would want to save her."

Robyn's heart twisted. "It's not just my mom," she insisted. "It's like a dozen people. All taken by Crown." Her tone sounded defensive, and she knew it.

Those other women *were* there and could be helped. But mostly, Mom.

"I know," Laurel said in a voice heavier than her

body. "But Key's right. I don't see how we can do it now, with the checkpoints and the crackdown."

The girls climbed a fire escape and darted over rooftops to avoid a roadside ID station staffed by a trio of MPs. The city buildings were close enough together that they hopped easily from one to the next. They laughed, enjoying the freedom and the grand bird's-eye view of the city. Flying above the MPs radar felt good, too. Everything seemed easier up high.

"I think I have a way," Robyn said. Roof tar pebbles crunched beneath their feet. "Have you heard of the Iron Teen contest?"

Laurel's eyes lit up. "Of course! I can't wait till I'm old enough to enter. I'll totally win. I'm like a ninja!"

She knifed her hands through the air in an elaborate chopping pattern. Then, as if to put the case in point, she vaulted over the three-foot gap between two rooftops, then tucked and rolled her way through the landing.

Robyn followed suit. "Right. So I heard two guys talking this morning. They said something about winners going to Castle District."

"For the finals," Laurel said. "If you're in the top six at the Sherwood contest, then you compete for citywide. In Castle."

They lowered themselves off another fire escape and onto a Dumpster.

"And," Laurel added. "You get to go to a fancy dinner at—" Her eyes popped wide. "THE GOVERNOR'S MANSION!"

Robyn's low spirits began to soar. This was the answer. She'd get to Mom, and fulfill her lifelong Iron Teen dream in the process.

≪CHAPTER FIFTEEN≫

Into the Lion's Den

"I can't believe I let you talk me into this." Key glanced nervously around as they stepped into the plaza in front of the Sherwood County central office complex. "It's insane. This place is crawling with MPs."

The ring of buildings included Sherwood's county offices, the Sherwood County Courthouse, the Tax, Loans, and Finance Building, and Sherwood Police Headquarters, which currently had a banner tied over its sign that read Military Police Headquarters. Instead of flying the usual Nott City emblem, now the pole in the plaza flew a black flag with a silver crown emblazoned on it. Crown's logo was like a pirate flag, Robyn thought.

"They might make you take off your glove," Key warned. "What then?"

Robyn glanced at his hand. He had taken a more permanent solution to the Tag problem. The back of his hand bore a rectangular black tattoo, obscuring his bar-code. She wondered, not for the first time, what he was hiding. But then, he probably wondered the same about her. Their true identities were still their own secrets.

"I won't let them scan my Tag," she assured him.

Key glanced at his blackout spot. "If they try to look at my hand . . ."

"It's going to be fine," Robyn said. "Trust me."

"Ha. Right," Key said with a broad grin. "As if."

"Ouch, that hurts." Robyn winked at him. She smiled inside. Joking about not trusting each other felt like some kind of progress. What they had might not have been trust, exactly, but it was close.

Robyn and Key headed toward the central building, where Sherwood's elected representatives had their offices. At least, they used to. With Parliament dissolved, Robyn wondered what was happening to the district staff. Was Crown controlling them? Replacing them with his own people? A rebel leader should really know these things, Robyn supposed. Tucker probably did. Maybe even Key. They knew how to ask the right questions and gather information. Unlike her. That's what made them a good team.

"Into the lion's den," Key muttered. He stuck his Tag hand in his pocket as they crossed through the tall glass doors.

$$\text{\ggg}\!\longrightarrow$$

Five floors above, Sheriff Mallet stalked through the halls of Sherwood MP Headquarters. She slammed a knuckle into the Down elevator button like it was a punching bag.

Seven trucks, stolen. Practically before breakfast.

The report had reached her desk an hour ago. It would be her duty now to report it to Crown. If he hadn't already heard, through the official grapevine.

Mallet would make the call. She had to. But first, she needed to think.

The elevator dinged, marking each passing floor. Her mind spun as she rode down to the second sub-basement. She strode into the lab where a dozen forensic techs were hard at work, running scans and testing samples lifted from crime scenes.

The techs scrambled to attention when she walked in.

"Progress report," Mallet barked.

The lead tech rolled his ergonomic chair back from the lab counter and spun toward the sheriff. His gloved hands held a silvery orb the size of a golf ball.

"This hologram unit is stubborn," the tech said. "We are two-thirds of the way in."

"It's taking longer than I expected," Mallet informed him. She wasn't sure whether to be relieved or annoyed. She settled for feeling relieved but acting annoyed.

Mallet continued to war within herself. Revealing her suspicions about the girl's real identity might speed her capture. But on the other hand, it put Mallet at risk for revealing that she had known too much too soon—that she had failed on the Night of Shadows. Crown would have her job for that. No promotion. No power. Back to the streets.

Mallet suppressed a shiver. She smiled calmly at the lab tech. "I'll await your report."

Back in her office, she immediately drew up the relevant case files. Loxley. Mother: Lucille Anderson Loxley. Father: Robert Loxley. Both suspected leaders in the renewed rebellion effort. Both apprehended.

Daughter: Robyn. The one who got away during the roundups. Mallet had managed to conceal the error. She stood by that choice. The serious mistake on her part had been not doubling down on the search for the girl. Not making sure it was taken care of that same night.

Humiliated. By a child. Mallet brushed off the thoughts as she scrolled the records for the dozenth time, hoping for new clues to emerge. The transcripts spoke of a restless child. Intelligent. A troublemaker.

The file contained a few school photos from years past, none recent enough to be useful on a Wanted poster. The girl was a teenager now. The sketch on the new Wanted posters came from MP eyewitnesses from the showdown at the fairgrounds. Mallet had seen the girl herself that day, and the sketch looked good to her.

Priority one was to catch the girl before her identity could be revealed. Protect herself from having to face the music.

Mallet sighed and punched the intercom. "Get me Crown," she ordered.

Her assistant's voice rang through moments later. "Shiffley's office holding for you."

Shiffley's office. Mallet grimaced. So Crown was continuing to pawn her off on his chief of staff. That did not bode well.

Shiffley—and Crown—had always underestimated her. Her success counted on always being better than the men. Stronger, smarter, faster. Perfect in the execution of her duties . . . or maintaining the illusion thereof.

She closed the Loxley case file, rolling her shoulders as she reached for the phone. She could handle the pressure. There were always tough decisions. She made them without blinking. She was, in every way, the right woman for the job.

≪CHAPTER SIXTEEN≫

The Fine Print

Robyn and Key walked, big as life, into the Sherwood District central office building. The lobby was quiet. And empty, except for a reception and security desk straight ahead, and two banks of elevators, one on either side.

The security guard took one look at them and said "Iron Teen? Second floor, make a left." He handed them plastic badges, which were blank except for the word *visitor*, the number 2, and a simple barcode. "Use it in the elevator, under the laser reader," he added in a bored voice. Exactly the opposite of Robyn's fear that they would be immediately recognized, scooped up, and imprisoned. But it was too soon to feel relief.

They took the elevator to the second floor, padded down the gray-and-white linoleum corridor to a door labeled Iron Teen Office. It was a small room, with one man in a cubicle and several empty chairs. The man, hunched over his computer terminal, barely looked up.

The machine was off-white in color, like most desktop computers Robyn had ever seen, but it had an engraved plastic plate mounted above the top of the screen that read C.

"We're here to register," Key said.

The man opened a file on his computer screen. "Name and age?"

"Key Johnson. Sixteen."

The man typed quickly, then shifted his gaze to Robyn. "And you?"

"Roby—"

"Roberta," Key interjected, cutting her off.

"Last name?"

"Roberta . . . Calzone," Key said.

"I'm twelve," Robyn added. She supposed Key was right—a fake name was best for something like this. She'd been planning to use a false last name anyway, though she would have chosen something better than Calzone.

"Johnson, you're 472; Calzone, 473." He struck a button, and the computer printer began humming and jerking.

Hundreds of entrants? Robyn was shocked. In Castle District, hardly anyone paid attention to the Iron Teen contest. The contestant pool was rarely more than a hundred. Obviously Sherwood was different. A thousand Points meant more to people here, while everyone who entered in Castle was doing it mostly for fun.

Back home, Robyn had thought she stood a decent chance of winning, but now, she was not so sure. Against hundreds? What was she even doing here? Was any of it worth the risk?

The registration coordinator grabbed the printed pages from the tray and handed them over. "This is your number. This is your training group. Report to this building at 10:30 a.m."

From a drawer in the desk he pulled two thick stacks of paper and placed one in front of each teen. "This is your contract. Basically says you understand the rules, won't hold the city at fault if you break a leg on the course or anything. Standard clauses. Sign and date on the back." He slapped an ink pen on top.

The contract spanned many pages, and the typeface was quite small. Robyn flipped through it casually. Did it matter what the contract said, since she was signing a false name? She understood the rules of the Iron Teen tournament. It was easily the thing she'd paid most attention to in the months before the Night of Shadows.

Every paragraph was about something different. Iron Teen contestant ROBERTA CALZONE (hereafter referred to as "Entrant") . . . blah, blah, blah . . .

Rules. Entrant must be between twelve and sixteen years old at the time of registration . . . blah, blah, blah . . .

Liability. Entrant understands the contest course is physically strenuous and participation may result in injury . . . blah, blah, blah . . .

Military Police Academy. Entrant agrees to be considered a candidate for enrollment in the Military Police Academy . . . blah, blah, blah . . . Like that mattered. Robyn wasn't about to join the Military Police.

She also didn't want to waste time reading the fine print. Too cumbersome. She was impatient to simply get on with the show. She took the pen and signed her new name, big and bold: *Roberta Calzone*.

"Calzone?" Robyn chided Key as they walked back toward the cathedral. "Do I look like an Italian pizza pocket to you?" She wondered if maybe her face had broken out. The idea had to have come from somewhere.

"So sue me," Key said, looking a tad chagrined. "I was hungry."

"It has a certain ring to it, I suppose. I certainly won't forget it."

Key snapped his fingers. "See, there you go. Argument one in favor of 'Calzone': memorability. Obviously, I was thinking of it that way all along."

"Obviously." Robyn nudged him with her shoulder. Key nudged back.

The moment they got back, Laurel bounced through the office door with excitement. "We have to start your training right away," she chirped. "I can be your coach!"

"We also need to get some fake parents on standby," Key informed her. "The contract said you need either a number or a parent to confirm your entry."

Fake parents? Robyn felt a flicker of heat in her belly. That's what the whole thing was about. Getting Mom back. Her real mom. But she knew what Key meant. It wasn't rational to be annoyed at him.

"Parent or guardian," Robyn said aloud. "We can use Tucker, or someone from T.C."

"What do you need a parent or guardian for?" Scarlet asked, strolling into the office to join them.

"We signed up for the Iron Teen contest."

Scarlet froze. Her cheeks paled. "What?"

Laurel resumed her celebratory dance. "We're going to win Iron Teen and go to Castle. I mean, Robyn is. Or Key. But probably Robyn. Sorry, Key."

Scarlet's expression grew more and more alarmed. Her cheeks flushed, matching the red tips of her spiked black hair.

"You can't sign up for Iron Teen," Scarlet exclaimed. "Please tell me you didn't sign yet."

"We already registered," Key confirmed.

"Why? What's the problem?" Robyn asked.

"Oh no," Scarlet said. "No, no, no, no, no." She began pacing short rows in front of them. "I can figure a way out of this. I can do it," she muttered.

Key and Robyn glanced at each other in alarm.

"What's wrong?"

Scarlet shook her head. "Iron Teen is what's wrong. The contest—it's a mess. It's a trap. You can't win."

"We can win," Laurel piped up. "You haven't seen our tricks, so you don't know."

"No one wins at Iron Teen, is my point." Scarlet was growing more agitated.

"We don't have to win, just place high," Key explained. "We'll have a chance to release some of the prisoners who were taken on the Night of Shadows."

"The top six Sherwood finalists go to the governor's mansion," Robyn said.

"And Points!" Laurel chirped. "Lots and lots of Points!" She was clearly dazzled by the idea of winning money for acrobatics.

"That's not all that happens to the winners," Scarlet said, her voice heavy. "You didn't read the fine print, did you?"

Robyn's stomach began to churn. "What are you talking about?" Whatever Scarlet was about to say, it was worth the risk, she reminded herself. For the chance to get to Mom.

Scarlet didn't answer.

"What?" Robyn said, more urgently. "Tell us."

Scarlet nodded. "I'm not going to tell you. I'm going to show you. Don't leave."

The black-and-red-haired girl turned and darted out of the sanctuary. The plywood clapped behind her.

Robyn looked at Laurel and Key. "Well, that was cryptic."

≪CHAPTER SEVENTEEN≫

The Sixth Element

Scarlet returned less than an hour later to find the others sitting cross-legged on the altar, playing cards.

She wasn't alone.

The young man with her was tall, sandy-haired, green-eyed, and . . . strangely familiar. He was dressed casually; that was the difference. He looked normal because he was not wearing his . . .

Robyn gasped as recognition clicked.

She jumped to her feet. She didn't feel it happen; her body simply rose on the surge of anger and terror that overtook her like a tsunami wave.

"You brought an MP here?" she cried, incredulous. He was the same young MP Robyn had encountered several times in the past. He had arrested her!

Scarlet held up her hand to stall Robyn's complaints. "This is Jeb. My boyfriend."

"Your boyfriend is an MP?" Laurel burst out.

"That might have been nice to let us know," Key said. The two came to stand behind Robyn in solidarity. Was their perfect hideout blown?

"I never brought him before because I knew you'd react that way. But now I had to."

"I helped Scarlet escape from Sherwood Jail, remember?" Jeb grinned. "Or, I would have if you hadn't already been there breaking people out."

"I remember," Robyn said. She had wondered more than once about the connection between Scarlet and the young MP. But she had been kind of busy to worry about it lately, plus she and Scarlet were still only barely friends.

"So he figures he owes you one, after that," Scarlet said.

Jeb put his arm around Scarlet. "More than one." He kissed the side of her face.

Robyn crossed her arms and tapped her toe, the picture of petulance. "Explain."

"Jeb competed in Iron Teen last year."

"Yeah," Jeb said. "You have to understand. It's not really a contest for fun. It's a recruitment tool for junior MPs."

"So what?" Robyn said. "It was in the contract, that you can join the MP training academy."

"No. You don't join. You get conscripted," Scarlet said. "It's not like they leave it up to you."

"How can they do that?" Key demanded.

"It's in the fine print," Jeb explained. "Winners, finalists, and any other contestants they choose. Basically anyone who performs well in the contest."

Robyn shook her head. "I don't care. They can't make me be an MP."

Jeb gazed at her sadly. "Trust me. They can."

Robyn got a chill down her back at the sorrow in his voice. She wanted to ask what he meant, ask how he knew, but she couldn't get out the words. Maybe she didn't really want to know.

"There's only one thing to do," Jeb said. "You have to throw your performances."

"Lose on purpose? No way," Robyn said. Giving up Iron Teen meant giving up the chance to find her mother. It might be the best chance she'd ever have. Castle District—and the governor's mansion, especially—was locked down tight, according to Merryan's report. It would be impossible to get in there on their own.

"So we just don't show up," Key said with a shrug. "Problem solved."

"If you register and don't show, they'll investigate you," Scarlet said. "That happened to someone we know."

"We gave fake names," Key reminded her. "They'll never find us."

"But they'll be looking," Scarlet said.

"They're already looking. We can't give up," Robyn insisted. "It might be our only chance to get to Castle District."

"One of us *might* get to Castle. It was a long shot to begin with." Key's cautious pessimism was not helping the situation.

"And how are we supposed to get the rest of us there?" Scarlet said.

"We'll figure something out," Robyn said.

"That's what you always say," Key answered.

Robyn glared at him. "And that's what we always do."

Long stare, silent pause.

Robyn couldn't bear the stillness for long. "I don't care what you want to do. I'm going to compete."

Key leaned back in the chair. He fancied himself some sort of hoodlum kingpin, Robyn imagined. Always the one behind the desk. Always the one in charge. But the chosen one from the curtain message, the daughter of shadows and light? That was Robyn. She was supposed to be the leader. She was the one who got to choose.

Key sighed. "After everything, you're still in it for yourself."

"Why shouldn't I be," Robyn snapped, "if no one else is going to help me?"

"That's not fair. You can't get everything your way all the time. That's what happens when you're part of a group."

Robyn had never been part of a group. She was an only child, and used to getting her own way—however she had to get it. Even for small things, like staying up past her bedtime. Now, when the stakes were higher— life or death, jail or free—it was all the more important.

"I have to do this," she said softly. "Even if it's on my own."

Key dropped his gaze to the broad surface of the desk. He sighed. Robyn wondered what he was thinking. If he had ever wanted anything as badly as she wanted to find her mom. If he could feel that longing radiating from her skin like the heat of a thousand suns.

Robyn pressed her hand over her heart. She could feel the pendants resting on her chest through her shirt. As always, they gave her strength. Kept her calm.

Key wiped his brow as if relieving a layer of sweat. But the room was too cool for that. "Yeah, okay," he said.

"I can tell you all about how the contest works," Jeb said.

"It's foolish," Scarlet said.

"Not if we don't win," Key said.

"Or even compete well," Jeb said. "You don't have to win to be conscripted. But you're right. They won't want weak MPs."

Key nodded.

"We report for our training session in a couple of days," Robyn said. "It's at the central office building.

Maybe we can still use the contest to create some havoc for Mallet."

"Steal something from inside?" Laurel said eagerly.

"Or hack their system from within," Scarlet suggested. "I can write you some code to upload. We can get a back door into their system."

"If we sneak into their server room?" Robyn asked.

"Yeah."

"Risky," Key murmured.

Scarlet and Robyn exchanged a glance. If there was one thing they saw eye to eye on, it was taking crazy risks for the greater gain.

"So I'll do it," Robyn offered. "You stay with Iron Teen and cover for me."

Key remained skeptical. His brow furrowed.

"It's good for the cause," Scarlet promised. "We can get all kinds of useful info off their system."

"Things we can use against them?" Laurel piped in.

"Exactly." Scarlet's gaze grew distant, as if she was already writing the code in her head.

"The office building isn't highly secure," Jeb said. "Getting in is the hardest part . . . so that actually could work."

"Okay," Key agreed. "Get on it. We'll figure something out."

"Yeah." Robyn tried to echo his authoritative tone. If she wanted people to listen, she was going to have to speak tough.

Scarlet was already pecking away at her tablet.

This was a great plan, Robyn thought. One thing she was good at for sure was causing trouble for the powers that be. And now she had more time to convince her friends to go through with the rest of the plan. She *would* win Iron Teen and get back to Castle.

"I guess I'll be going," Jeb said. He touched Scarlet's shoulder and walked toward the door.

"Jeb," Robyn called after him. She didn't plan it. The question bubbled out of her spontaneously, like a cough. "What's your Element?"

"I'm air," he answered quietly.

"And shadow," Robyn said, stepping toward him.

"That's the one we're missing," Laurel exclaimed. "You're one of us!"

Jeb nodded, almost reluctantly. "Possibly."

Robyn turned to Scarlet, who was staring at the floor. "You knew."

Scarlet raised her head. "I was waiting for the right time."

"You knew we needed to complete the Elements," Robyn said. The group had talked about it several times. The shrine curtain's message made it clear that all the Elements had to be gathered. Six friends—and up until now, there had only been five.

"I couldn't assume he was your sixth Element," Scarlet said. "Lots of people are air."

Right. But not that many people had helped Robyn out of more than one jam already, before they even became friends.

"We can't keep things from each other."

Key snorted a laugh. "Look who's talking."

Robyn glared at him. "Shut up."

Key kept on grinning. Robyn said nothing. They had found the sixth Element.

The curtain's prophecy was coming true.

She pushed down the worries that came with that thought. Focus. Jeb had the inside knowledge she needed to win.

A flicker of satisfaction ignited itself inside her. Obviously her Iron Teen plan was meant to be.

≺CHAPTER EIGHTEEN≻

Calzone, Anyone?

The Sherwood District central office building looked as gray and intimidating as ever. A banner out front read, Welcome, Iron Teen Contestants! The cordon of MPs lurking around the sign made the atmosphere less than welcoming, in Robyn's opinion.

Robyn stroked the back of her glove and hoped the covering wouldn't be questioned.

It had worked at registration, which lasted all of five minutes. They were going to be in here for two hours today. She had her red beret on, plus a pair of blank-lensed, brown-rimmed glasses Tucker had dug up from somewhere in the cathedral basement.

Robyn took slow deep breaths to try to calm down.

"Try to relax," Key whispered as they approached the building. "You're starting to look like you need medical attention."

Robyn slugged him in the arm. He laughed. "There you go. Spirit of competition. Much better."

The exchange successfully broke the tension. It reminded Robyn she wasn't alone—if something went wrong at least Key would be there to know about it.

They entered the district office building. The bored desk officer informed them, "They've moved the training next door." He pointed through a set of glass doors leading to an enclosed walkway.

"Thanks," Key said politely, and they headed for the correct door. Under his breath he muttered, "Well, there goes our plan."

"Bummer," Robyn agreed. Key looked distressed, much more so than Robyn felt. He was only in it for today. She planned to go the distance.

Fresh stencil work on the glass read Military Police Headquarters, with a little forward arrow. Robyn and Key looked at each other. Training in the MPs' headquarters?

Gulp. Talk about the lion's den.

There was no door at the other end of the walkway; the corridor simply opened up into the lobby of MP headquarters. Robyn found herself staring at a wall of Wanted posters. The imagery was growing far too familiar. It was all she thought about, much of the time; she didn't exactly need to face it in person. She turned away, but trying not to look like she was purposely turning away, she sought out something to study on the other side of the room.

The lobby was painted stark white, with steel and silver accents. Scattered islands of white cushioned couches and gray curtains added up to the feeling of being inside a cloud. *A dark, stormy cloud*, Robyn decided.

So this was where the MPs hung out.

The place seemed fancy—for Sherwood—but plain at the same time. Another of Crown's black and silver pirate flags hung behind the reception desk. The desk itself was high, like a bar, and painted black. Two MPs in leather chairs had a console of video cameras beside them, a computer each, and a bank of phones that looked capable of launching the building into outer space. Robyn craned her neck to see the computers as they passed.

The guards were very focused on the computers and hardly glanced at the security monitors at all. Robyn noted this with a small smile.

The rest of the space was full of teenagers, some small and lithe, others muscled and hulking. They all looked out of place in the orderly, grown-up surroundings.

Robyn and Key approached a folding table near the elevator bank, labeled Iron Teen Check-In. The table was covered in official-looking papers, but there was no one sitting at it. The crowd of contestants around didn't really seem to be in a line, so Robyn and Key went right up to the table.

A woman in a lavender pants suit stood beside the table. She had her back to them, studying a thick file folder open across her hands. A dark knot of hair bundled at the base of her neck.

Robyn cleared her throat. "Excuse me, we're here to check in?"

"They'll be right back," the woman said. She turned around. It was Marissa Mallet—the sheriff herself.

≪CHAPTER NINETEEN≫

Sheriff's Handshake

Robyn let out an involuntary yelp at the sight of the sheriff. She clapped her hand over her mouth, trying to hold it back, but it was too late. "Oh, uh, you startled me," she managed to say, after a long awkward silence.

Mallet's dark eyebrows slanted into a V. "I can see that."

"I, uh, didn't expect to see you in person. It's kind of surreal," Robyn admitted. True enough. Her brain rattled with conflicts as she tried to will down every impulse. The anger. The fear. The questions. *Where are my parents?* she wanted to scream. *Do you know?*

"Welcome to Iron Teen," Mallet said. Her severe expression softened into a smile. Not a friendly one, but a smile nonetheless. A sharp gleam rose in her eyes—recognition?

Robyn feared the worst. They'd stood face-to-face

once before. Today her braid was safely tucked under her beret. She hoped the glasses formed enough of a mask to obscure her identity up close. She willed herself to hold her hands at her sides to keep from fiddling with the frames.

"Thanks," Key said, covering the speechlessness that overtook Robyn.

Mallet's eyes were still on Robyn. "It's always especially nice to welcome young women to the contest," she said.

Robyn nodded mutely as her brain spun toward mush.

"She's a very big fan," Key explained. "It's an honor to meet you."

Mallet smiled, with a little more feeling this time. "I'm glad to see girls like you taking an interest in this. Law enforcement is a great career option, if you're athletic and ambitious. Got to be a little bit of both," she said, smiling again.

Law enforcement? It was true that Iron Teen contestants tended to be male, but there had always been plenty of female police officers, as far as Robyn knew. Although, Marissa Mallet was the first female sheriff Robyn had ever heard of in Nott City.

Mallet continued, "But girls need to know it's okay to achieve, you know?"

"Yes. I've been looking forward to trying this contest

for a long time," Robyn said. "Thanks for still doing it," she blurted. "Even though things are—I mean, with everything changing—I mean . . ." She glanced up at the silver crown flag, and let her voice trail off before she said something even stupider.

"It's more important now than ever, don't you think?" Mallet said.

"I suppose," Robyn murmured. At a loss for what else to say to a woman who scared the living daylights out of her, she stuck out her hand. "I'm Roberta Calzone. It's very nice to meet you."

Mallet enclosed Robyn's fingers in a cool, firm shake. "Best of luck to you, Roberta." Mallet's gaze sharpened on Robyn. "I have a feeling you're going to do all right. I'll be watching for you."

Great. Just what I need. Robyn hoped her smile didn't look as fake as it felt.

The harried-looking young man Robyn remembered from the registration office returned to his post behind the table. "Hi," he said. "Numbers?"

Robyn and Key held up the cards he had given them. "Your group is in room 27A," the registration coordinator told them. "Second floor." He pointed them toward the stairwell, through a doorway, which was guarded by a beefy, uniformed MP. They flashed their Iron Teen badges and he allowed them to pass.

$$\ggg\!\!\longrightarrow$$

Sheriff Mallet watched the pair of friends slip through security. Her stomach flipped with a butterfly sensation that closely resembled nervousness. It made no sense.

She had this situation under control.

The boy and girl disappeared into the stairwell. They seemed like good kids.

She'd barely looked at the boy, come to think of it. The girl had been quite magnetic. She had confidence and determination behind her eyes. She reminded Mallet of herself as a young girl. The awkwardness would wear off one day, exposing that wiry strength. All to the good.

Mallet's eyes narrowed. "Roberta Calzone," she murmured.

The face was perhaps . . . familiar. Apple cheeks gone slack with shock and nervousness. Parted lips. Wide, anxious eyes. Not exactly the face of a notorious rebel.

And why would she be *here?* Right in the MP headquarters.

Back when she was a beat cop, early in her days on the Nott City police force, she had learned to trust those knots of intuition.

She pressed the comm link on her PalmTab. "Send some officers down," she ordered her assistant. "I need to locate two Iron Teen contestants."

》》⟶

Robyn and Key emerged from the stairwell on the second floor and headed down the corridor, looking for room 27A. The hallways upstairs were much emptier than the lobby, but still bustling with MPs, Iron Teen contestants, and other office workers.

"That was . . . ," Key whispered.

"—Freaky?" Robyn finished. "Yeah."

"I can't believe she didn't recognize us." He shook his head. "At least you're on her good side, for now."

"Well, Roberta is, at any rate." Robyn and Key laughed tensely as they entered the room marked 27A. About a dozen other teens occupied the room, sitting on beige stackable chairs arranged in an oval circle.

"Hello." A large, pretty girl in a red-and-orange dress greeted them. She had a very silky bob of dark-brown hair, and hazel eyes that sparkled. Robyn struggled to suppress the grin that spread across her face at the sight of her.

The other girl smiled, too. "I'm Merryan," she said, offering her hand for Robyn. "I'm the controller for Group 27."

"I'm . . . Roberta," she said. Merryan's familiar smile had made her almost blurt out the truth. The girls shook hands. Robyn marveled at how being in charge made Merryan seem taller than usual. She was nearly as tall as Robyn to begin with, but her timid manner often made her seem to shrink.

"Come on in, Roberta," Merryan said. She turned to Key. "And . . ."

"Key," he said, sticking out his hand. "Key Johnson."

"Nice to meet you."

Key smiled, though it seemed a bit strained to Robyn's eye. What was Merryan doing here? It couldn't be a coincidence.

"Well, come in, both of you. We're about to get started."

Key beelined for the far side of the room, but Robyn lingered by the door, wanting to get the lay of the land. None of the other contestants seemed very impressive, physically, though Robyn supposed she didn't appear that way to them, either. She wouldn't underestimate anyone, that was for sure.

"Do you always go by Roberta?"

"What?" Robyn turned to Merryan, who was marking their names off on a clipboard. "Um, you can call me 'Robbie,'" she said, making up the nickname on the spot.

"Oh." Merryan smiled. "Good. I guess 'Roberta' seems very formal, or something."

"I've always thought so, too," Robyn murmured. The game of not knowing each other was kind of fun.

Merryan turned to address the whole room. "Well, it seems everyone is here now." She consulted her clipboard. "First things first, I'm required to go over the rules of the contest."

Around the room, people groaned. "Yes, I know," Merryan said. "We all know the basic rules, but it's important for contestants to hear everything officially, so there's no confusion."

Robyn headed over to take a seat beside Key. Merryan read through the official rules. *She has a pleasant voice,* Robyn thought, tuning out the actual words. It was hard to pay attention, because the longer she sat in MP headquarters, the more she realized this was a prime opportunity. Somewhere in this building, there must be computer terminals with the highest clearance, and full access to the MP's prisoner database. If she could get out of this room somehow, maybe she could still complete something of their plan . . .

"No tools, knives, or weapons of any kind will be permitted on the field," Merryan was saying. "You are allowed athletic shoes and basic athletic clothing. No cleats. No hats. No sunglasses."

Robyn's mind snapped to attention.

No hats!

She involuntarily fingered the edge of her beret. This hat protected her braid. She always wore it when she wasn't busy thieving. The intricate braid her father had taught her made her very recognizable as the one and only Robyn Hoodlum.

She *had* to wear the beret. And she *had* to compete.

Something had to give.

⊰CHAPTER TWENTY⊱
The Plan

Sheriff Mallet returned to her office, having dispatched two MPs to locate the children. She sat in her tall white chair and leaned back against the headrest. She closed her eyes.

The building was lousy with Iron Teen hopefuls. It could take some time to locate the two. Let the officers comb through the team records.

She could wait.

She could plan.

"Bring them to me quietly," she'd said.

"Okay, let's head downstairs," Merryan said. Everyone stood up.

Robyn leaped up, startled. Had she missed something? Where were they going?

"We'll have an hour in the training room," Merryan said as she led the group into the hallway. "It'll just be us, and a few MPs to explain the various elements."

Oh, that made sense. Robyn wished the contestants were allowed to practice on the actual Iron Teen course. But part of the challenge of the tournament was that the course was unknown and everyone would be seeing it for the first time during the preliminary run.

Merryan led the group toward the elevator bank.

"How'd you land this gig?" Robyn asked her casually as they walked.

"Oh, I'm an intern," Merryan said. "There are a bunch of us. I'm from Castle." She held up her gold lanyard and used it to key into the elevator. "I guess the idea is to keep it unbiased. This way, they can be pretty sure people from other districts don't have friends among the contestants." The pretty girl blushed. "Not that it's bad to have friends from Sherwood," she stammered. "I mean, I don't, but only, I mean not because—"

"I understand," Robyn said, cutting her off before she could break character. She smiled and winked. "I can honestly say I don't have any friends from Castle District, either."

Merryan laughed. "Okay."

They took an elevator to the basement, where what

appeared to normally be a cafeteria had been transformed into a training facility. Monkey bars, climbing
ropes, tire rings, balance beams, tumbling mats, rock
walls, elevated metal platforms . . . The room looked
like a mishmash of a gymnastics arena and an auto-
body shop.

A few months ago, Robyn would have been thrilled
at the sight. It should have been a dream come true, to
be so close to the day she had been imagining forever.
Except for those strange metal platforms, Robyn knew
perfectly well how to deal with every challenge present. Climbing ropes? Monkey bars? Piece of cake. But
Robyn couldn't focus on practice right now.

Two MP guards stood in the center of the mats with
their hands folded behind them. They looked ready to
enforce the rules. Robyn edged her way to the back of
the group. In a minute they might be asking her to take
off her beret. She couldn't let that happen. Not here.

While Key and everyone else clustered closer to the
equipment, Robyn quietly walked the perimeter of the
practice area. She tried to act like she was looking at
the various elements, but really, she was looking for a
way to slip out of the room unnoticed.

In the original plan, Robyn was supposed to sneak
out at this point. Key might want to act like an ordinary
contestant now, but Robyn didn't. Being in MP headquarters instead of the office building wasn't enough
to deter her efforts. She checked to be sure no one was

looking, then pushed through a set of wide, swinging doors.

The kitchen equipment stood silent, unused. Robyn wove her way past a stand mixer that was practically as tall as she was and shelves full of sheet pans and stockpots the size of tree stumps.

A bright-red Exit sign pointed the way upstairs.

MP headquarters had four floors, not including this basement. Robyn figured the computers with highest clearance would be on the highest floor, so she headed straight up. She was right. So right, in fact, that she couldn't even get into the fourth floor from the stairwell. The door had a digital keypad and a card-swipe slot.

Robyn jiggled the handle, but nothing happened. She punched in random codes, and was rewarded with nothing but an insistent flashing red light.

The third floor enjoyed no such protection. Robyn just walked in. She spotted several security cameras trained on the hallway, but she had expected that.

Robyn glanced at the security camera and thought about the desk guards downstairs. No way could they be watching all the cameras at once, if they were even paying attention at the moment. Maybe no one would notice her. She was sure she could be out in a matter of moments. Iron Teen contestants were arriving in shifts, so it wouldn't look too weird for her to be wandering around in the building.

There were very few people on this level, though, considering the hundreds of teens downstairs. A few MPs and office staff members popped up here and there. None of them looked twice at Robyn, though. *Act like you belong, and no one will question it.* She started to relax.

Then she turned a corner and nearly ran headlong into someone wearing an MP uniform.

"Oh, excuse me," a familiar voice said. Then the man grabbed her arm and yanked her around the corner swiftly.

At first all she could see was the MP cloth and slender brown hands. He maneuvered their bodies through a narrow doorway and into a dim enclosed space, then pushed up against her as the door shut behind them.

Robyn pressed her hands against his chest to get some space. She jerked her head upward to see the man's face. It was Jeb.

"Crap, you scared me," Robyn cried. "What are you doing?"

"I saw you on the monitors. I blocked the screen from the others. What do you think you're doing up here?"

"Infiltrating. Get off me."

"Well, I can't, really," said Jeb. He had one hand on the closet doorknob and one on the back wall. It was a janitor's closet, so the floor space was largely occupied by industrial-size buckets, mops, brooms, and jugs of brightly colored solutions. A single bulb in the flat, fluorescent panel overhead lit the space.

"I mean, can we get out of this closet?" Robyn said. "If I'm with you, they won't think anything of me being up here, right?"

"Not exactly," Jeb said. "I'm not supposed to be on this floor, either. Being seen with you could blow my cover."

"So forget you ever saw me. Just tell me, which way to the server room?"

Jeb sighed. "I came to warn you. I tried to cover the monitor, but someone might've seen you. My unit just received a possible intruder alert." He checked his watch. "Scarlet's jamming the security camera feed for the next four and a half minutes. If the cameras are down longer than that, extra protocols come into play. But it should be enough time to get you back to the training space."

"I can't." Robyn pointed to her head. "No hats allowed on the course."

Jeb frowned. "This was a bad idea."

Robyn was incensed. "This was the plan!"

"If we were in the office building, yeah." Jeb ran a hand over his hair. "Here, you're putting us all at risk."

"It's worth it," Robyn said. *Anyway, I'm the only one risking everything,* she thought. *No one asked you to come and help me.*

"Go left from here. Take the back stairs toward the subbasement. No guards. No door, either. There's a window at the ground level. It'll be tight, but you can fit."

With that, Jeb pushed out of the closet and the door drifted shut behind him.

Robyn waited a few seconds before following. The coast was probably clear by now. If someone caught her, she could claim she'd gotten lost looking for her Iron Teen training room. Robyn peeked through the door windows of each empty office she passed.

Four minutes. That was quite a bit of time, really.

Robyn reached under her cap for a hairpin. Laurel had taught her plenty about lock picking in a pinch.

The computer terminals in each cubicle were basic and unencrypted, but they were still part of the internal network. If she planted Scarlet's code here, maybe they'd still be able to do something with it.

Crunch! The sound of an industrial stapler punching through a sheaf of papers echoed, loud as a gunshot.

A propped-open door led to an adjacent office. There was someone in that room! A desk light was on in one of the cubicles, and the staple was followed by a cough and shuffle.

Robyn couldn't see the person, which meant they couldn't see her. All she had to do was stay low and quiet.

As she bent over the keyboard, Robyn heard the tell-tale creak of door hinges—directly behind her.

"The contestants in question are no longer with their group," the MP said into his intercom.

"Lock the building down," Mallet answered.

≺CHAPTER TWENTY-ONE≻

Answers

Robyn whipped around, prepared to make a run for it. It was too late to hide—the door was already opening.

Key poked his head in from the hallway. "Robyn? Get out of there, someone's coming!"

"What are you doing up here?" Robyn demanded. The relief that flooded her burst out angrily. She clicked over the keyboard, typing the sequences Scarlet had trained her for.

"I followed you," Key said. Behind him, Robyn heard voices in the hallway. Key slid the rest of the way into the room and closed the door behind him. The voices grew louder and the frosted pane of glass in the door reflected dark moving shapes as the talking people passed by.

"What are you thinking?" Key hissed, pressing himself against the wall. He reached down and pressed the door-lock button, something Robyn hadn't thought to do.

"This is MP headquarters," Robyn said. "I knew somewhere in here there'd be a computer with access to the same network."

Key shook his head. "The original plan is blown. We're here for Iron Teen." He glanced at her beret. "But I guess that's blown now, too."

"It'll just take a minute," Robyn said. She looked through the open door again. This time, she caught a glimpse of the other worker. A heavyset man in a sweater vest stood by the printer, pulling pages off the rack. Robyn ducked out of sight, annoyed. What was this guy doing at work on a Saturday morning? Didn't he know he was cramping Robyn's style?

Key ducked alongside her, still talking. "At best, you'll get us kicked out of the contest. At worst . . ."

Robyn knew perfectly well what was worse. "I have to find them," she said. Scarlet's hacking might turn up info about her parents. Mom was being held in Centurion Gate, at the governor's mansion, but what about Dad? And all the rest of the disappeared rebellion leaders? Robyn stared up at the ceiling as if she could see through to the upper floors. "The answer is here, somewhere."

"Iron Teen," Key emphasized. "We have to get out of it without drawing attention to ourselves. And then we can get on with business as usual."

"But—" Robyn's protest died on her lips as a dark blur filled the glass on the hall door. The knob rattled as a key worked the lock. Key yanked Robyn's arm, and they dove farther beneath the desk of the empty cubicle.

The door swung open, then clicked shut again. Footsteps shushed across the carpet. Chair springs groaned as someone settled in at another desk. Then the electronic whir of a computer powering up.

Key tapped his wrist, holding it out to Robyn. Their practice hour was almost up. Not to mention the four minutes of camera static that Scarlet had arranged.

And Key didn't know there might already be MPs gunning for them. As if on cue, a soft ringing alarm sounded overhead. *It was an almost pleasant sound,* Robyn thought. Maybe the whole fugitive thing was starting to feel a little *too* good . . .

"That's probably for us," Key said.

"Definitely for us," Robyn confirmed. "Let's boogie."

On the other side of the felt divide, fingers clicked against the keyboard. There was really only one choice. Time to go.

They jumped up and ran back into the hallway. The time for stealth was over.

"Hey," the startled worker cried as they burst past him.

"If you'd told me, we could have made a new plan," Key said, when they were out.

Key and his big plans, Robyn thought. Sometimes, you just had to seize an opportunity.

"There wasn't time. We didn't know we'd be in MP headquarters," Robyn said. "I wasn't going to pass up the chance."

But Key had made her pass up the chance. If he hadn't barged in and startled her, she would have gotten into the system.

Robyn could kick herself for allowing Key to distract her. He didn't understand what she was going through. There was no way he could know how she felt. All Key cared about was the movement, and surviving in the here and now. Robyn wanted her old life back, and the only way was through finding her parents. Both of them. And it would help the Crescent Rebellion, too. Once the captured were free, people might stop looking to Robyn. They could get a real leader. Someone with experience and authority. Like her mom and dad.

"I'm not saying give up," Key said. "I'm saying this isn't the time."

Whatever, Robyn thought as they hurried through the hall. *You just don't understand.*

Iron Teen mattered to her; it did. So did the rebellion. But it was nothing compared to how she felt about finding her parents. Thinking this now, she felt a tiny pang. Iron Teen was a problem, a challenge. The rebellion was full of even bigger problems. Rescuing her parents—that was a solution. It was the only thing in front of her that felt like an answer, instead of more questions.

As she led Key toward the stairwell Jeb had pointed out, Robyn grew nervous. She would fit through the narrow window, but Key was larger. *There's always a way out when you're small*, Laurel liked to say. Slipping out of the cafeteria had been easy, and Robyn hadn't worried about getting back or getting out. She could make her way just fine.

She glanced at the boy beside her. Why had he insisted on following her? Everything was different when you had to think about someone besides yourself.

"That was a bit close, eh?" Scarlet said. She crouched outside the stairwell window as Robyn and Key crawled out.

"No time for small talk," Key blurted out. "Run!"

Robyn and Scarlet followed at a casual pace.

"Not really cut out for stealth, is he?" Scarlet remarked.

"Scares easy," Robyn agreed as their blond compatriot scurried out of sight around a corner. "How'd you find us?"

"Jeb." Scarlet held up the tablet she carried everywhere. "I have this, and MPs all get PalmTabs."

"You can just message him? Like normal?"

Scarlet shrugged. "He's not under surveillance, and I'm pretty far off the grid."

They caught up to Key.

"Didn't anyone ever tell you running looks suspicious?" Scarlet smacked his arm.

"Easy for you to say. You weren't inside," Key breathed.

Scarlet arched a brow. As if she hadn't been on the inside plenty of times.

Key stood staring into a window full of real estate listings, acting like he was shopping for a luxury condo.

"We've got a perfectly good cathedral," Robyn teased, tossing up her hands. "But someone's always in the market for an upgrade."

The three paused then. It was hard to resist the draw of real, furnished living quarters. The shiny, clean images lasted for a few fleeting seconds, then pixelated out and were replaced by others. Similar to the way the Wanted posters scrolled.

"Let's get out of here," Key said.

"Someday," Scarlet said, touching her fingertips to the window screen. They turned and walked away.

≪CHAPTER TWENTY-TWO≫

The Big Chop

Robyn was still determined to compete in Iron Teen, despite the pesky little matter of the no hats rule. And despite the possibility that the sheriff and the MPs were onto them.

"We should've realized earlier," Key said. "You can't very well wear a beret in the competition. That would look strange."

"You tried," Tucker said. "That's all you could do."

"It's not over," Robyn blurted out. "We still have the contest. We still need to get to Castle District."

Key glanced at her slantwise. "We can't go back now. You introduced yourself to the sheriff."

"It seemed like a good idea at the time," Robyn mumbled. Now it seemed extra dumb. What had she been thinking?

"Surely we're on camera, running around up in there, too," Key added. "They'll have a perfect image."

"Scarlet looped the feed," Robyn said. "How good are security camera images usually anyway?"

"It doesn't matter," Key said. "There's no way you can go unnoticed with that hairstyle."

"I could try to braid it differently." Any kind of braid might draw attention to her, though. She had seen Mallet face-to-face twice now—the beret and glasses had let her get away with it today, but she didn't trust the subtlety of different braid styles.

"Or wear it down," Laurel suggested.

Robyn shot her a look. "Not likely."

Key shrugged. "What? It's probably cute. Super curly, right?"

That was the understatement of the hour. "It's enormous. It would literally get in my way."

"Bun. Knot. Updo. Ponytail?" Laurel chanted.

Robyn shook her head. The younger girl's hair hung like straw. She didn't get it.

"So we call it quits," Key confirmed. "Put our energies elsewhere."

Robyn twirled the end of her braid in her fingers. Unless . . .

Robyn stood in the basement shower room and studied herself in the mirror. She breathed long and slow, preparing.

No hesitation. Just go.

The scissors felt cold across the base of her neck, as the blade gnawed through the thick braid like a rope. The web of her thumb ached. Her knuckles, all knotted, complained. She flexed her fingers in the scissor rings, determined.

Everyone makes sacrifices. Dad's voice in her head. *The trick is to know for sure what it is you want most.*

Closing her eyes, she squeezed and sawed until the last hairs separated with a tiny jolt that startled her. Her scalp tingled with relief as all tension released and the braid came loose in her hand.

When it was free, she laid it reverently on the edge of the sink.

Slowly she unwound the remaining locks along her head. Then she took the scissors and lopped off long chunks, snipping close to her scalp.

Dry, the short hair stuck out in awkward directions. It appeared matted and poofy at the same time, somehow.

When she emerged from the shower, her hair was soaked and curling like a cap against her skull. *It didn't look so bad*, she figured. *Kind of cute, really.*

Still, the tears rolled as Robyn swept the floor and wiped down the sink, gathering and discarding her lifelong locks. The long tail of the lopped-off braid, she saved. It was a part of her. Something she couldn't easily throw out.

Upstairs her friends stared at her in shock.

"I wasn't sure you'd really do it," Key said. Robyn couldn't tell if he was impressed or annoyed. She knew he was ready to scrap the Iron Teen idea and stick with their normal thieving.

Robyn looked at him, hoping the firmness of her gaze would remind him: she would do anything for the chance to find her parents. Anything.

"You look way different," Laurel said, circling Robyn.

"I know." Robyn patted her bare neck. "It feels weird." *Like a part of me is missing.* But that was par for the course these days. Missing her hair, she realized now, was not the same kind of ache as missing her parents.

"It's a good disguise," Key admitted. "You don't look much like the hoodlum anymore."

Robyn rubbed her neck again. "That's the idea."

"So, no more heists until after Iron Teen." Key's suggestion seemed practical. But Robyn had already thought of that.

"Now I'll wear berets on the heists," she said. "To keep my nonhoodlum disguise in place." She held the braid inside the back of the beret. It would be easy enough to sew it in later. When she plopped it on her head, Laurel giggled. "Now you look like you again."

Robyn grinned. "Exactly." *They'll still know it's me.*

$$\text{\ggg}\!\longrightarrow$$

A daytime heist was the height of hubris, but when opportunity knocked, Robyn and gang always opened the door.

It helped to have an MP insider on their team. Shortly after they left the office complex, Jeb had messaged Scarlet with some upsetting news.

"Well," Scarlet had told the others. "We've figured out where they're taking some of the things they've confiscated from local businesses. You're not going to believe it."

"Another impound lot?" Key speculated.

"Worse," Scarlet said. "They're opening a big-box store on the Cannonway. Kind of like the new grocery depots, except with clothes and household things. Run by MPs, staffed by Sherwood people who need to pay off debt."

"What?" Laurel asked. "They're going to resell the things they stole?" She stood in the center of the room with her fists planted on her hips. Her voice rose to a near shriek. "Not. Okay."

"Of course they are," Robyn groaned. "We could have seen that coming."

"Clothes, electronics, housewares, furniture," Scarlet rattled off the list, reading from her tablet.

Robyn picked at the ragged T-shirt she wore. In fact, she had been wearing it for a couple of days now. "My wardrobe could certainly use an overhaul," she commented. They each had only a few items that they scrubbed clean with bar soap every week.

"We need to go shopping,"

"Okay," Key said readily, "ı

The three girls looked at around. Clearly outnumbered

"No one knows about th.

them. "It's completely unsecured. ɪɪ ɪɩ .. ..

bunch of inventory, but guards won't be in place until tonight."

"So we go right now," Robyn confirmed.

As usual, breaking in was not the problem. Breaking out unnoticed was where the trouble came in. Either Jeb had relayed the timing wrong, or the guards had arrived early to get themselves situated.

They ran. Out of the box store, through the crowds.

"Remind me again, why did I think it was good to be recognizable?" Robyn said. She puffed out the words between gasps. They could *not* be caught. Not now.

Laurel giggled. "We got this." The girl barely seemed out of breath, despite their fast pace and the bulging sack she carried over her shoulder.

"No security, my tailbone," Key grumbled. "If we make it out of this alive, remind me to kill you later."

"Hoodlums coming through!" Scarlet shouted as they darted among clumps of unsuspecting pedestrians.

ound seams in the crowd easily enough.
them, the MPs shoved people aside, trying to
up. "Time to split," Laurel announced as they got
rther down the Cannonway, where there were fewer
pedestrians to provide cover.

"See you up top!" Robyn answered. The four friends fanned out and raced in opposite directions. The MPs would have to part to follow them, and one person at a time would be harder to spot in the crowds.

Robyn zipped off the Cannonway to a parallel street and started heading in the opposite direction. She yanked off her beret and slowed to a walk. When she was sure no MP would see, she ducked into an alley and climbed the nearest fire escape. She leaped from building to building across the rooftops toward the place they had planned to meet.

When she got there, Robyn found Laurel standing casually at the edge of the roof, brushing her teeth. Robyn laughed.

Laurel held up a tube of toothpaste she must have grabbed during the heist. "This is the *good* kind." She beamed through the foam.

"Okay, Miss Oral Hygiene." Robyn smiled.

Scarlet arrived moments later, just in time to watch Laurel spit a white glob in a high arc over the roof ledge. "That's nasty," she said.

"That's minty," Laurel corrected, wiping her mouth with her fist and pocketing the toothpaste.

When Key arrived, they laid out their haul—four garbage bags full of assorted clothing. It made sense to bring only what they needed back to the cathedral. The rest they could pick up later and deliver to T.C.

"Fashion show!" Laurel declared. She stripped down to her tank top and leggings and threw on outfit after outfit, modeling them for the others. Most of the items were comically large on her. The others sat on the roof stones and watched, calling dibs on things that caught their interest, amassing small piles of treasure.

Laurel danced and played, flapping too-long sleeves and flipping up collars to mug like a deranged private eye.

It was amazing really, how easy it had become to appreciate the simple things. Small, tangible things, like clean shirts and toothpaste. And the invisible things that were not so small to Robyn anymore, like laughter, and a brief moment of feeling completely safe, completely free.

The sun sank in the sky, but they stayed on the rooftop anyway. Robyn never wanted the day to end.

≪CHAPTER TWENTY-THREE≫

Preliminaries

Sherwood Park was almost unrecognizable. All decked out for Iron Teen, the place had been transformed. Over the top of the check-in tent, wooden bleachers stood up tall enough to be seen from several blocks away. The whole setup appeared nearly as large as the sports stadium in Notting District. At the stadium, everything was indoors. Here, it was all outside and spread out, a small city of tents, booths, and tables.

"Check in at the registrar," Robyn heard no less than a dozen times as she and Key made their way through the crowd. Iron Teen interns and volunteers wore yellow shirts, with a giant IT on the front and back. MPs were everywhere, mingling and herding the hordes.

The long registrar table had a dozen computers on it, with workers behind each. Robyn and Key stood in line. Scarlet's red-tipped spiked hair poked up from behind the table. She appeared to be functioning as some kind of tech intern, scrambling around among a nest of wires and cords on the ground. Robyn tried not to catch her eye.

"Next."

Robyn and Key stepped up and presented their registration cards. The registrar glanced at Robyn's gloved hand. "Tag?"

She shook her head. The gloves would have to come off for the race, but she would keep the protection on as long as possible.

He sighed and punched a couple of extra buttons. "Sign here." As if showing up without a number was an annoyingly common occurrence.

Roberta Calzone, Robyn scrawled. The *e* in Roberta looked a bit funny, because her hand had automatically started to write a *y* after *Rob*, but she figured the signature was passable.

The registrar barely even glanced at it. He handed her paperwork to the intern beside him, who filed it into a bin. A senior MP drifting by in the background paused, raised his hand toward Robyn, then moved on.

The registrar handed her a timing belt to hook around her wrist or ankle. The stretchy wrap had a computer chip in it that would keep track of Robyn's time. With almost five hundred contestants, they had to start the race in shifts. Scoring wasn't just about who physically crossed the finish line first—it was about who had the best course time start to finish.

Robyn received tracker 401. Key got number 72.

"They start you in groups of fifty," the registrar informed them. "Proceed to your assigned tent. Your group leader will send you out to the starting zone when it's time."

"We can't start together?" Key asked.

"Next," the registrar repeated, looking behind them. "Uh, no, the numbers are randomly assigned. No team-work allowed."

Key seemed disappointed, but Robyn secretly felt a bit relieved. If they didn't start together, she wouldn't have to feel bad about leaving him in her dust.

The senior MP's fingers flew over his PalmTab:

Roberta Calzone has checked in.

Sheriff Mallet received the photograph on her desk screen. Cute girl. Smiling. Brown skin. Crowned with a ragged mop of short, swirly curls.

Dang.

There had been no mystical braid under the beret.

Let her go.

Mallet responded to the officer, then leaned back in her chair. She closed her eyes, thinking. Hunches were hunches. They didn't always pan out.

It made no sense, anyway, why the girl would put herself out on a limb, in plain sight. For the reward money? The Iron Teen purse was a hefty sum for most teenagers, but so far the hoodlum seemed more clever than greedy.

Mallet opened her eyes. The girl had sparked a feeling of recognition, perhaps for a different reason. Yes. The hunt for the hoodlum was clouding the sheriff's judgment. Everyone seemed like a suspect. Not so. The girl had expressed interest in law enforcement, after all. She was a fan. It had felt nice, Mallet recalled, to be admired. Perhaps the feeling of kinship had been one of a mentor to a possible mentee. The girl's performance in the contest would clarify it.

Mallet swiveled her chair toward the intercom button. "I've changed my mind," she told her assistant. "Show me the live feed."

The desk screen lit up with multiple camera angles of the festivities in Sherwood Park.

If Roberta Calzone made it into the top fifty, she'd prove herself worthy of the sheriff's attention. Mallet smiled. Today's events just became a lot more interesting.

Key and Robyn followed a winding path through the tents and emerged onto the open field. For the first time, Robyn saw the extent of her competition up close. Hundreds of teens, looking determined and fit, shaking out their limbs to keep the muscles warm.

"How many are there?" Robyn mused.

"About five hundred, didn't we figure?" Key answered, sounding equally awed.

Their group tent was nothing but a canvas roof on poles, with all four sides open to the air. "Hi, Robbie; hi, Key," Merryan said cheerfully as they ducked under the awning and took a seat on the grass in one corner. She handed them bottles of cool water, and they sipped dutifully. It felt like they'd barely been sitting long at all when Merryan started calling out groups. "Zero to fifty . . . Fifty to one hundred . . ."

"Well," Key said. "Guess I'll see you on the other side." They slapped hands.

"Good luck," Robyn said. She stared out at the other contestants. Many seemed so much bigger than her. Not that it mattered. She was limber and fast, but the idea of the race didn't feel as exciting as it should. Over the top of the tents, she could see people high in the bleachers waving their arms and cheering. She could hear the cheers, but not the ones she wanted to hear.

She had never imagined competing without Mom and Dad there to cheer her on. The path to the finish line would be long and lonely knowing they wouldn't be there to greet her at the end. Surely Laurel was up there somewhere, shouting at the top of her lungs along with everyone, but it wasn't the same.

"Robbie?" Merryan said. "You okay?"

The use of the fake nickname jolted her mind out of

its wanderings. "Huh? Yeah. Is it time?" Robyn glanced around. She was the only one left in their tent.

"Almost. You'll be next," Merryan confirmed. "I just asked if you wanted to stretch or warm up or anything. You're sitting very still."

"I—I guess I'm just nervous," Robyn admitted.

"Nerves are good for you," Merryan said. "It means you're all focused and ready."

Robyn's heart tightened. She dropped her head onto her knees. "My mom used to say that."

Merryan nodded. "So, it must be true then, huh?"

Robyn stared at the grass. "She would touch my cheek, and she has these really graceful hands . . ." It felt strange, to be telling another girl something so personal. But Merryan's gentle expression made Robyn want to tell her more. She longed to ask if she'd returned to visit the dungeon, but in this crowd someone could too easily overhear.

"You sound so sad when you talk about her," Merryan said. There was more to be said, but she couldn't.

"She . . . I haven't seen her in such a long time," Robyn admitted. Every minute, not knowing, felt like hours, or days. She couldn't help whispering, "Is she okay?"

Another contestant from the group veered close to them. Merryan couldn't answer, except for a slight half nod. "I think so," she whispered back, when they were more alone. But they weren't really alone, so Robyn would have to settle for that teardrop of information.

"My mother died a long time ago," Merryan said.

"I'm sorry," Robyn whispered. "It's terrible that she's gone, isn't it?"

Merryan nodded. "Do you want to tell me something else about your mom?" she said softly.

Robyn thought about it. "She always came to watch me compete," she said. "One time, after I had a really bad gymnastics meet—" Robyn shuddered at the memory. It had been truly awful, she'd screwed up her vault, tripped in the floor exercise, fallen off the balance beam and bruised her shoulder and almost cried in front of everyone. "It was really terrible, and I got the lowest score, but Mom was there and she just said, 'You're my winner. All the time.'"

"That's cool," Merryan said.

"Yeah," Robyn agreed. And surprisingly, she felt better, because even though Mom was out of reach, she was surely thinking about Robyn. Thinking of her as a winner. She could make Mom proud, even from a distance.

"It's about time," Merryan said. "Are you ready?"

"Ready as I'll ever be," Robyn answered, stripping off her gloves and dropping them into her bag. Merryan clasped Robyn's bare hands and helped pull her to her feet. Their fingers squeezed against each other longer than necessary. Robyn drew strength from the grip, resisting the unusual instinct to throw her arms around the other girl.

"Go get 'em," Merryan whispered, in a way that made Robyn wonder if she knew Robyn now planned to perform well. She tugged her hands free.

Here goes nothing, Robyn thought as she strode out of the tent toward the starting line.

⊰CHAPTER TWENTY-FOUR⊱

Iron Teen

Robyn crowded among her starting group on the grass between the bleachers. The crowd roared above. She looked for Laurel, not really expecting to locate her one small face in the masses. She waved anyway, just in case Laurel had spotted her.

The starting line was merely a spray-painted stretch of grass with electronic boxes at either end to record the time on each racer's bracelet. It would also be the finish line. She looked behind her, to try to get a glimpse of the final obstacle, but the other end of the arena was blocked off by a giant curtain. The course designers had clearly thought of everything; it would just have to be a surprise.

The whistle blew, and the mob of contestants started running. They raced across a long stretch of grass, first as a pack, then pulling apart as faster runners took the lead and slower ones fell behind. The staggering of groups was necessary, Robyn realized, because as they rounded the first curve, the course narrowed until it was only wide enough for about ten or twelve people at once.

The obstacles came one after the other. She traversed a balance beam over a bed of water and stones. Rope-swing over a slushy moat from one ceramic island to the next.

An uphill jog along a paved street ended with a twenty-foot wooden wall built into a hillside. The wall was a maze of ladders that began and ended randomly so Robyn had to jump, swing, or stretch from one to the other. It led to a slick slide down a tall-grassed slope on the other side. The trail was lined with plastic or rubber—Robyn couldn't tell which—but it was stamped with the toy-company logo of the obstacle's sponsor. A real-life Chutes and Ladders?

Robyn rolled to one side to avoid a pit of sand near the bottom; she didn't want to land in that slow mess!

Next came wooden pedestals suspended above an inch-deep oil slick; Robyn jumped from one to the next like a frog on lily pads. Sponsored by your friendly neighborhood oil and lube technicians. Robyn thought it was funny that all the obstacles had ads and sponsorship. Did they really think she might be considering an oil change right now? Perhaps the ads were meant for the people who might be watching on TV.

Robyn vaulted over a series of three-foot walls made from boxes of powdered detergent, sponsored by Lancaster Laundry. She high-stepped through a maze of empty tires, belly-crawled through a plastic tube with accordion folded walls, and swung across a trail-wide set of monkey bars that felt like they would never end. Sponsored by Nott City Zoo, each bar proclaimed proudly.

Robyn's adrenaline fueled her forward motion. She felt like she was flying. She passed several people moving so slowly that they just appeared to be dangling there. Luckily she spied the mud trap at the end of the bars, so she finished her final swing fast and released the bars with no hesitation. The momentum carried her right over the three-foot-wide bowl of murky sludge. It smelled like . . . well, like something you might find beneath a monkey bars in the zoo. She stumbled her way out of the landing, but ran on. Others who weren't so lucky crawled out of the pit behind her, soaked and dirty.

Robyn tore across a gravel lot, along with several others. She could see the top of the bleachers in the near distance. She had to be getting close to the end. Around the corner might be the last obstacle. As she turned, her pounding heart sank. She found herself approaching strange metal platforms, the very thing she hadn't taken time to figure out during the practice session. Uh-oh.

The platforms were each about the size of a passenger van. There were eight of them, staggered in a cluster blocking the trail, and they were *moving*. Up and down, forward and back, tilt and flat, a combination—each one seemed to operate at its own rhythm. A rapid, consistent rhythm. Other contestants dove at the nearest, lowest platform, but Robyn stopped and stared. Clearly it was necessary to jump from one to the other to get past them all, but what was the best order?

The low platform rose quickly, but it tilted suddenly and half the people fell off. Robyn realized she needed a higher platform. She took a deep breath and vertical leaped as high as she could to reach the highest platform. She pulled herself up, then ran forward and flat-flipped straight over a lower, tilted level onto one that was spinning in a slow circle. From there she jumped down free and clear and raced into the stadium toward the finish line.

From her office, Sheriff Mallet watched split-screen coverage of the contest. She jotted down various chest numbers of the contestants she favored. The Calzone girl was performing particularly well.

Mallet poked one corner of her screen and drew up the contestant files. Roberta Calzone. No Tag, so the details in the file were sketchy. A poor girl from Sherwood, blessed with nothing but determination and skill. Rising from nowhere to become someone. Mallet smiled. Yes, she could work with that.

She had speed, endurance, agility, flexibility . . . but Mallet narrowed her eyes as she studied the footage. Something was amiss.

The girl coasted across the monkey bars as smoothly as if she were walking down the street. Excellent form.

It was the dark spot on the back of the girl's hand that raised Mallet's hackles again. She double-checked the file. Calzone. No Tag.

But the footage was clear. Roberta Calzone did have a Tag.

Robyn waited breathlessly for her time to pop up. Her assigned number, 401, blinked on the "Finished" Board. After a seeming eternity, it disappeared, and reappeared on the leader board. Position nine! She cheered inside. The crowd behind the barricades cheered, too. So she'd been wrong that no one would cheer for her at the finish. But these people didn't know her. Perhaps they had been cheering every time a new number appeared on the leader board.

Merryan came running over to Robyn. "You made it! And you're in the top ten," she gushed. "This is so exciting."

Robyn followed wearily, relieved that at least one

person wasn't giving her a hard time about making the finals. The adrenaline buzzing through her system tapered off. She was tired and ready to rest.

Seeing where they were headed, though, Robyn felt a new surge of energy—one powered not by happiness but by fear. Merryan dragged her toward a stage full of MPs, including Jeb and several others.

Robyn swallowed hard. She'd known that just competing in the contest had been a big risk. But the exposure of victory had even bigger drawbacks, Robyn suddenly realized.

Merryan led Robyn into an area near the stage with the other top fifty winners. Of course, the race wasn't over yet, but it would be very soon. By the end, Robyn was bumped down to tenth place, after a contestant from the final starting group bounced into the number two spot. Robyn dutifully cheered as he joined the finalists' lineup.

Robyn studied the screen, searching for Key's number. He must've finished long before now, but he was clearly not in the top fifty. He'd played it slow, like Robyn was supposed to do.

She sighed. Her friends were not going to be too happy.

"Check all the finalists' Tags," Mallet ordered.

"We're not set up to do that," the senior MP told her. "They're already being given instruction sheets and sent on their way."

Mallet simmered over this information. Who was Roberta Calzone? One of the next generation of great female MPs? Or, indeed, the hoodlum in disguise?

Mallet could afford no mistakes. She needed to be certain. Beyond a shadow of a doubt.

"We can try to round them up," the MP offered. "We can probably get most of them back."

Only twenty-four hours until the final round. It wouldn't do to stir up the crowd, and make people aware that something was out of the ordinary.

"No. We wait," Mallet said. "She'll return to us of her own accord."

≪CHAPTER TWENTY-FIVE≫

Reunion

Robyn scampered away from Sherwood Park. Everything was going according to plan. *Her* plan, anyway. She wondered what would be in store for her back at the cathedral. Key would be frustrated with her, but she pushed those worries aside. He would come around. Or else she'd proceed on her own. All things felt possible.

Robyn spotted a familiar face darting among the crowd. That scar was distinctive, not to mention the scowl. Floyd Bridger!

"Bridger!" Robyn cried out.

The man flinched. He spun around fast and hurled himself into the shadows at the same time.

Robyn ran after him into the dim alleyway. "Wait."

He barked at her angrily. "Where did you hear that name?"

"On your Wanted poster." Robyn gasped for air to fill her lungs. "We met once; we have your things."

Bridger's eyes widened in recognition. "You. You're the girl from the crowd. The day they tried to—" His expression relaxed. Surely he remembered how Robyn had thrown herself at two MPs to allow him to break free as they tried to arrest him. She expected him to say more—a thank-you, or an explanation—but he only stared down at her.

"Yes," she said. "We've wondered what happened to you." There wasn't much more to say. She wasn't sure, suddenly, why she had even called out to him.

"I've been hiding out in the other counties mostly," Bridger told her, surprising her with the truth. "Now, with the stricter lockdown, I'm trapped back in here."

"I suppose you have me to thank for that, too," Robyn said.

"You're the hoodlum?" he said, looking disdainfully at her.

"You seemed like a nice man that day," Robyn said, feeling disappointed. This gruff attitude was not. "What happened?" Part of her wanted to walk away, but she didn't. She couldn't explain why she felt drawn to talk to him. Like Chazz, he was intimidating and magnetic at the same time. And dismissive—his almost-sneer seemed eerily familiar.

"Don't underestimate what these people can do to you," Bridger said softly. "They've taken everything from me."

Robyn wondered about the weight behind his words. "They've taken from me, too," she said. "From all of us. That's why we're fighting."

Bridger scoffed. "What you're doing ain't fighting," he said. "You call me up when you find the fire."

"I'm it," she said quietly. "I've already gathered the Elements." Robyn surprised herself, too, by speaking about the real situation. That almost never happened. Who was he, and why did it matter?

Bridger looked closer.

"You ain't found your fire," he said. "Not a flicker."

Robyn knew he meant to insult her. She tried not to take offense. It was true, wasn't it? She'd thought so herself. "I'll find it," she said. "I'm going to save everyone." The words blurted out, practically of their own accord. They tasted odd. Why had she even said that. It sounded so grandiose.

"The wisdom of the moon shrines promises us a fire. It has all happened before. It will all happen again."

"Why do these prophecies even matter?" Robyn asked.

"They are not prophecies," Bridger said. "They are explanations. Our holy texts. Messages of hope. As long as the words are lost, so are we."

"The words aren't lost," Robyn told him. "We've read the curtain."

"You don't know what you're talking about, girl. The moon lore was under attack. Its followers, driven underground. When the shrines were built, the curtain was divided."

"Divided?"

"There's not one shrine, one curtain. There are three. There was a map, but it's long been believed to be destroyed."

More shrines? On the map? Her dad's map?

"Well," Robyn started to speak, but she paused. She didn't know Bridger, or that any of what he was saying was true. It felt true, but what did that mean in the real world? Only she and Laurel knew about Dad's map, and it was safest to keep it that way.

"You still have my things?" Bridger asked.

"Yes. We saved the whole backpack, exactly as you left it."

"Open them. There are things you can use," he told her.

"Don't you want your stuff back?"

"We'll meet again, if we're meant to." He turned and ran off down the alley.

Robyn lay in the bell tower and hugged the radio to her chest, listening to Nessa Croft's soothing voice and thinking about Bridger's comments. She had barely gotten around to accepting that she was a freak child, with some mysterious destiny. Why did there have to be more and more on top of it? One shrine wasn't enough? What was she supposed to do, find the rest of them? Bridger might've had all the time in the world to chase moon lore myths, but Robyn had other things to do. There were too many current puzzles to waste time with ancient ones.

Her TexTer vibrated. Another anonymous message.

Iron Teen? Way too risky. Stop it now.

She had never responded to the anonymous texts. It could be a trap. Her thumbs moved of their own accord, fueled by frustration. *You don't know me. Leave me alone.*

If I can find out, they can find out. Stop.

Robyn pushed the TexTer aside. Once again it felt like she was being asked to let go of the thing she wanted most. To release her parents into the ether of lost things.

Robyn hid for a while in the cathedral bell tower, the one to which she alone held the key. She didn't know yet how to face the others. They'd be angry with her for going out on a limb. She would make them understand, somehow. Or else she'd be on her own again.

She drew up her knees and faced the painted arrows and names on the wall. They were around her, outside her. Together they formed a group, yet she was not exactly part of it. All she had was herself. The way it had always been. It wouldn't do to forget that. Ever.

"You saw him?" Laurel exclaimed. "For real?" Her eyes bugged wide as Robyn related the story of running into Bridger.

Robyn led Laurel down into the moon shrine.

"The curtain was torn," Laurel said. "So there's more to the prophecy?"

"I guess," Robyn said. "We have to figure it out."

"Tucker will know. We should ask him."

"I will, eventually." She stared at the curtain. "First I want to see what we can come up with."

Robyn pulled out the map her father had left for her. The old parchment was worn at the edges and the creases. The symbols were important, she knew, but what did they ultimately mean? "What do we know?" she whispered, half to herself.

Laurel bobbed enthusiastically on the stones. "There were originally three shrines—earth, air, and water. They were separated into a triangle to represent the tip of the arrow." She held her pointer fingers and thumbs together.

"How do you know that?" Robyn asked, surprised.

Laurel shrugged. "Tucker talks A LOT."

Robyn smiled. "What else?"

"The moon lore symbolism follows the arrow. There's the tip, then the shaft, and then the feather, and it all represents the six expressions of the Elements: dark/air, light/air, dark/earth, light/earth, dark/water, light/water."

Robyn nodded. This part was familiar. "Six expressions, but only three Elements. Three parts of the arrow."

"Six when you add shadow side and light," Laurel speculated.

"Yeah," Robyn mused.

"And then there is a fire at the heart of it all," Laurel added, with a frown. "But I don't know how that fits into the arrow."

The map came alive under Robyn's eyes then. She could see the arrow, so blindingly clear that she was surprised she'd never noticed it.

"I don't get it," said Laurel. "What are we looking at?"

Robyn traced her finger over the arrow pattern for her friend.

Laurel's eyes lit up. "What does it mean?" she asked.

"I think it means we're not finished," Robyn answered. "There's more to the moon lore message."

"The arrow," Laurel said. "What does it point toward?" She dragged her finger off the edge of the map, following the arrow's trajectory. "What's over here?"

"Castle District," Robyn answered. "It points toward Crown."

Laurel's eyes widened. "Are we going to shoot him with an arrow?"

"Yeah," Robyn said quietly. "I suppose we are."

≪CHAPTER TWENTY-SIX≫

Breakthrough

The lab tech's voice trembled with some combination of nerves and excitement. "We can see the girl," he told the sheriff. "Still working on the ID."

"I'm coming down," Mallet responded.

"No need," said the tech. "Here she is."

From the surface of her desk screen, the hologram appeared.

Mallet leaned back in her chair. The girl's silent shadow spun slowly in front of her, mouthing words of rebellion.

Determination. Grit. A sly tilt to her lip.

Robyn Hoodlum was definitely Roberta Calzone.

"You did too well today," Jeb said.

"I wasn't trying to win," Robyn said.

"You did just well enough to squeak by into the finals. On purpose, right?"

Robyn didn't meet his eyes.

"Whatever you're thinking about doing, rethink it," Jeb said quietly.

"The longer I'm in the contest, the more access we have to the Sherwood District building." She wondered if the lie sounded as transparent to him as it did to her.

"I've told you, they won't take you back in there."

"Maybe things have changed since last year. They changed the training location, after all."

Jeb shook his head. "You've gotten lucky so far, with your small-time food thefts."

"Small-time?" Robyn echoed. "I don't think so. I refer you to my reward posters."

Jeb didn't crack a smile. "You know what I mean, right? It's one thing to pull a few clever stunts over on the MPs. Going head-to-head with Crown in his own backyard is straight foolish."

"Everyone else is happy with the outcome today."

"Try not to do any better tomorrow."

Robyn narrowed her eyes at Jeb's back. The guy wasn't nearly as dumb as his MP cohorts. She had been careful to be good but not too good. But Robyn had no intention of dialing back her efforts. She planned to step them up.

She was going to be in the top six. That free ticket to Castle District was hers for the taking. She was going to find her mother, even if she had to storm the governor's mansion all by herself to do it.

≺CHAPTER TWENTY-SEVEN≻

Trust

When Jeb left for the evening, Robyn felt relieved. The respite was short-lived. After their dinner together, Scarlet pulled Robyn aside.

"You're going to try to win, aren't you?" Scarlet asked.

"It's a bad idea, you said," Robyn answered, but she didn't meet the other girl's eye.

"What happened to that thing about not keeping things from each other? Don't you trust me?"

"Do you trust *me*?" Robyn shot back. The girls glared at each other, the glint in their eyes made them once again feel more like adversaries than friends.

"Enough has happened," Scarlet said slowly, "that . . . yeah. I guess I do."

Robyn was taken aback. Scarlet was the one always at the edge of the team, never putting herself in harm's way. Half the time, she straight-up disappeared.

"Okay," Robyn said. "Trust."

"Are you going to try to win?" Scarlet repeated.

"Yes," Robyn admitted.

"Then you're going to need this." Scarlet held out a small square of white paper with black squiggles on it. It looked like a Tag.

"It's a temporary tattoo," Scarlet said. "I designed it myself."

"Really?" Robyn was impressed.

"If you win, they'll transfer the money into your account by scanning your Tag."

"What about all the contestants who don't have Tags?"

"They have to prove their identity some other way," Scarlet said. "Probably some way that's hard to fake, like bringing in your parents and legal forms."

As if inventing a functioning Tag barcode wasn't hard? Robyn wanted to say. Instead she asked, "How did you make this?" She turned it over in her hands.

Scarlet frowned. "I've been working on it for months," she says. "Be careful with it. I don't have that many of them."

"You have *more*?" That was even more impressive.

"Well, they're all the same. I printed it from a computer. I only had so much tattoo paper, and I used most of it in testing. This one should work."

"And there's a fake bank account attached to it? If I win, we could actually get the reward money?"

"That part needs a little work still," Scarlet admitted. "But it will look to them like the money transferred, and that's good enough to keep you alive."

Robyn studied her own real Tag.

"How does it work?"

"Did you ever use SkinTint?"

Robyn tilted her head, surprised at the seeming non sequitur. "The costume paint?" She had a strong memory of being a green thing for Halloween one year. Her mother had painstakingly rubbed the green lotion over her face, neck, and arms. It came in all colors.

Scarlet nodded. "We'll get a shade that matches your skin and cover up your real tattoo. Then put this one over the top."

Robyn placed the white square over the back of her hand, tattoo side up, and protected it from sticking to her too soon.

"I—I don't know how likely it is that I can actually win," Robyn started to explain.

Scarlet smiled gently. "I promise not to tell the others."

"I want to get into the governor's mansion."

"If you get in, we're coming with you."

"How—?"

"I don't know," Scarlet said. "You're not the only one willing to do whatever it takes for a chance to free the ones who've been taken. We'll figure it out."

$$\text{\ggg}\!\longrightarrow$$

Robyn made her way to Sherwood Park for the Iron Teen finals. Wading through the crowds seemed lonely without Key. The audience was bigger, but the contestant pool was much smaller this time. Robyn felt exposed, even though Scarlet had rubbed her hand with SkinTint and the protection of the fake Tag was in place.

When she got to the check-in tent, she was relieved to see Scarlet there, working behind one of the check-in terminals. There was no line.

"Calzone," said the registrar. He frowned at his screen. "Your paperwork says no Tag, but there is a note here . . ." He squinted and clicked at the keyboard. "Some kind of error? Hold out your Tag hand."

Robyn put out her fist. The registrar passed the scanning wand over the temporary tattoo. Behind him, Scarlet's hands moved slower, untangling and twisting the wires with nervous deliberation. Waiting to see if her handiwork held up to official scrutiny.

Robyn refused to look at her directly. She mentally crossed her fingers.

"Roberta Calzone," Sheriff Mallet murmured. The Tag scan brought up a name, address, and a Points account with a very low balance. A scant sheet of records, to be sure, but not at all surprising for a random Sherwood girl.

"The Tag checks out," her lead MP commented over the intercom. "What was the problem again?"

Mallet stroked her chin, confused. She glanced at the hologram image of the hoodlum once more. The likeness had been close enough to convince her that Roberta Calzone was the elusive Robyn Loxley in disguise. There were differences. She could see them now. Perhaps Calzone's short, curly hair accented the shape of her face in just the right way to create confusion.

The sheriff choked down the now-familiar bolus of disappointment and relief.

"There's no problem," she told her man. "It was only a precaution. Let her compete."

In the prep tent, Merryan remained admirably in character, though she kept chewing her lip nervously and glancing at Robyn. Her gaze darted back and forth between Robyn's hands and face. Finally she reached out and wrapped her fingers around Robyn's wrist, pulling her hands apart.

"Stop picking at it," she whispered. And she was right. Robyn had been self-consciously poking at the fake Tag.

"If you win, you get to come to the governor's mansion for a victory dinner," Merryan said casually, as if

Robyn didn't know. "They bring all the Iron Teen winners together, actually. You might even get to meet the governor and everything."

"We've met," Robyn murmured to herself. She turned her head and found Merryan looking at her closely.

"Be careful," the girl whispered, shaking her dark bob. "They'll be watching the winners."

"I'm not supposed to win," Robyn reminded her.

Merryan smirked. "I know."

"It's unlikely."

"Right. 'Cause you're so good at doing what you're supposed to." Merryan gave Robyn's wrist a gentle squeeze.

Robyn gave her a side eye in answer. "If I make it there, can you still show me the way to the dungeon?"

"There are a lot of guards." Merryan glanced around, making sure there was still no one within earshot. She lowered her voice further. "But I went down last night. She's doing okay."

Robyn bounced on her toes, energized. "Thanks."

"Stay calm," Merryan reminded her, releasing her grip. But the steadiness of her touch had been comforting. Robyn quickly interlaced her fingers with Merryan's and held on.

Robyn's pulse pounded, fueled by a rush of adrenaline. *Save it for the course,* she tried to tell her body, but the excitement could not be tamped down. If winning Iron Teen could give her a chance to reunite with Mom, even through prison bars, there was nothing on earth that could stop Robyn from making it across that finish line at the head of the pack.

≪CHAPTER TWENTY-EIGHT≫

Downpour

It wasn't the earth that had it in for Robyn. It was the sky.

Running the Iron Teen obstacle course felt like nothing after the joy of finding out for sure that Mom was still okay. Robyn bounded through the now-familiar course, mindless of the other teens exerting themselves around her, and mindless of the blue-gray rain clouds gathering overhead.

The joined pair of pendants bounced against Robyn's chest as she ran, imbuing her with strength. A bit of Mom, a bit of Dad, and one very determined Robyn. *Offspring of Darkness, Daughter of Light.* Indeed.

Robyn scrambled up the staggered ladders. Sprinkling raindrops plunked down, causing her fingers to slip on the metal rungs. Every obstacle after this would be slippery now. The entire course made that much harder. Well, at least it would be harder for everyone else, too.

A little water never hurt anyone, Robyn told herself. She slid down the slide and took off running around the next corner. She opened her mouth as the rainfall intensified. Might as well hydrate.

She remained with the front pack of contestants, still determined to be among the first across the line. Her main competition appeared to be three boys. She recognized them from the top ten at prelims. The smallest of them, Robyn nicknamed "Speedy." He zipped like lightning from obstacle to obstacle but was slow to complete each challenge. Robyn and he passed one another repeatedly—she'd overtake him with acrobatics, then he would run past her on the straightaway.

That was fine. She couldn't afford to actually win—too much attention. All she needed was to make the top six. Third or fourth would be perfect.

One of the larger boys who had been keeping the lead tripped on the tire rings and crashed headfirst into the ground. He seemed to be getting up when Robyn hopscotched past, but from that point on, he stayed somewhere in her rearview. Speedy and the other boy moved on, still neck and neck with Robyn.

The rain wasn't even getting in the way that much . . . until she approached the series of hurdles sponsored by Lancaster Laundry detergent. The hurdles looked fine and normal, so Robyn approached them at top speed.

Speedy zipped past her, as expected, and launched himself at the boxes, as if he was going to climb over. Instead he crashed straight through. The air exploded with a shower of powdered laundry detergent. As the rain pounded down, it immediately began to bubble and foam.

Luckily Robyn wasn't directly behind Speedy, but she was already too close to the hurdle, and moving too fast to stop herself. She jumped, swung her legs into the air, and thrust her arm against the laundry detergent boxes to propel her forward. Her form was perfect; she performed the maneuver exactly how she'd done it in prelims. But, as Speedy had just demonstrated, soaking wet cardboard didn't hold up so well. Robyn's arm punched straight through, embedding itself to the elbow in powder.

The runner beside Robyn had tried a similar strategy. He slip-slid over the hurdle and landed with a splash in the burgeoning pile of foam Speedy's crash had created. He landed with such momentum that a wave of suds surged upward and splattered Robyn's side.

Robyn automatically ran a hand down her cheek to wipe away the goo. She rubbed the slick layer of detergent off her arm. As her fingers came away—so did a swipe of the SkinTint!

She started to panic. Rain alone wouldn't ruin her cover, but the detergent would. SkinTint came off easily with soap, and her fake Tag could be ruined.

Robyn rolled over the remaining hurdles as gently and quickly as she could. The soapy mess had slowed down the competition even more. Now the contest seemed to be down to just two—her and Speedy—who came out of nowhere behind her sputtering soap bubbles from his nose and ears.

As she ran, Robyn scrubbed her palms against her pants, trying to dry them in advance of the monkey bars. But falling off seemed like the least of her worries. Hopefully the MPs at the finish line wouldn't notice her blurred Tag and get suspicious.

The last stretch of the race went by in a blur. She had decided a long time ago—it was worth any risk to have a chance to save her mom. Key wasn't here to stop her. No friends would be harmed. It was Robyn and Robyn alone on the line.

She flew through the shifting metal platforms, barely thinking. She channeled all her speed into the final straightaway, knowing Speedy would sneak up behind her and overtake the lead.

He did. She heard his breaths behind her and smiled to herself. It was all going to be okay. Speedy bolted past her. The crowd gasped and surged—a collective groan from up in the stands. Robyn relaxed, prepared to coast in second.

Then, the unthinkable.

Speedy stopped. Or so it seemed. Robyn was suddenly three paces behind. Then two. And one, as Speedy went sprawling, limbs akimbo. Her momentum carried her past him.

Robyn crossed the finish line first. Her chest broke the tape, and she thrust her fists in the air and cried out with joy and despair. The crowd roared.

Robyn stared up at the giant TV screens mounted around the arena. Half of them were still tuned into the rest of the race, contestants scrabbling through mud, rain, and soap suds to get to the finish. The other half showed her face.

She fought the instinct to throw her arms up over her head. Seeing herself large on the screen like that, she realized winning came with a price. Her face was streaked and mottled with water, soap residue, and mud smears. Robyn stood, shocked and exposed, alone in the center of the field. Even without her braid, in a crowd of hundreds, someone was bound to realize the Iron Teen winner looked exactly like the fugitive, Robyn Hoodlum.

⫷CHAPTER TWENTY-NINE⫸

Gotcha

A girl winner. The sheriff could picture the newspaper headlines already, yet she knew it was never going to happen. Roberta Calzone burst across the finish line, her face a twisted mask of glory and pain. Camera flashes burst from all directions.

Mallet kept her eyes on the girl as she climbed the makeshift stage steps, prepared to crown the winner of the new Iron Teen Sherwood. She had come down from her office to preside over the brief closing ceremony. But not before seeing everything from above.

Amid the slip-and-slide of the contest's rainy surprise, something had caught her attention. Mallet had rewound the video and played it in slow motion. There it was. Just a glimpse. What was that, poking out of Roberta Calzone's shirt? A necklace?

Mallet froze the image, then smiled. A pendant. Familiar and strange.

This was no case of look-alikes, or mistaken identity. Somehow the hoodlum had deceived the system. Roberta Calzone was no Iron Teen hero. She was Robyn Loxley, traitor, thief, fugitive. That would teach the sheriff to ever doubt her instincts again.

The best news—the girl could be caught and named—without betraying Mallet's own mistake. She could announce that Robyn was, in fact, Roberta Calzone. No one would ever need to know about Mallet's mistake on the Night of Shadows.

The apprehension would be easy. Minutes from now, the fugitive would walk right up onto this stage, and into the MP's grasp. No reward would have to be paid. She could capture the hoodlum publicly, in front of all of Sherwood, and claim her rightful victory.

The sheriff couldn't have asked for a better outcome.

Merryan ran to Robyn where she stood in the center of the field, feeling less than victorious.

"You did it! Congratulations!" Merryan cried. She grabbed Robyn's wrist and thrust her fist to the sky. The crowd roared anew. Cameras flashed. Robyn turned away, but there was no away. Flashes came from all sides.

"I need to hide my face," Robyn whispered urgently. "Get me out of here."

Merryan led Robyn toward a covered tent at the side of the stage. "That was amazing."

"My hand," Robyn whispered urgently. "I have to fix it." The Tag was smeared beyond hope.

"What can we do?" Merryan asked, eager to help.

"I'm melting," Robyn said wryly. "Can't you tell?"

Merryan handed her a damp towel. "Sorry, everything got rained on," she explained.

Robyn scrubbed away the mud from her face. Split-second decision. She wiped away all the remnants of the fake Tag tattoo. The hint of deception would probably be worse than if they caught her real Tag.

"The SkinTint's in my bag," Robyn said. "Can you get it for me?"

"Your bag's all the way over in the starting tent. There's no time." Merryan rubbed at Robyn's skin around where the Tag had been. Between the muddy soap residue and the remaining SkinTint on the rest of her hand, maybe she could salvage enough brown to cover over the real Tag.

If all else failed, at least Robyn could pretend she was Tagless again. Except . . . they'd scanned her earlier! Uh-oh.

"Look, you have to go onstage now, Robbie," Merryan said, pointedly using the nickname. "You're going to get a medal."

Hearing the fake name jolted Robyn. She pressed her hand over the pendants at her chest. She whispered desperately, "I need Scarlet. Now."

Robyn felt her confidence draining away like the SkinTint.

"You don't get the reward until after the party," Merryan said. "It might be okay."

Robyn's nervous expression didn't fade.

"You could go to the bathroom, I guess. No one will think that's too weird after the race. And I'll go get—"

"Ready to go?" said a voice behind her. It was Jeb. This time, he was in uniform.

"Jeb—" Robyn started to speak.

He shook his head. "Come on, okay? They're waiting."

Jeb led her toward the stage. Robyn had no choice but to follow or draw further attention to herself.

"This way, Miss," Jeb said in a formal tone. He grasped her hand firmly, tugging her to follow him. Robyn fought the instinct to jerk her hand free. They were friends, sure, but the MP uniform nearly overpowered that connection. Just in time, she felt it—a cold, wet sensation where his hand was pressing against the back of hers.

He was replacing her tattoo!

Jeb led her to the stairs that led up onto the stage.

Marissa Mallet greeted Robyn. "Congratulations, Miss Calzone. I'll be so pleased to present you with the Iron Teen trophy and prize money."

Robyn nodded.

"And of course we're thrilled to have you as our newest enrollee at the Military Police Academy."

"What?" Robyn blurted out. "No, not yet."

Mallet smiled indulgently. "Surely you understood," she said. "Your entrance in the Military Police Academy is compulsory."

"Compulsory?" Robyn echoed automatically. In gymnastics, "compulsory" events were the ones you had to do to compete. Was Mallet saying Robyn would be forced to become an MP? Jeb had warned her of this, but it was supposed to happen later. After Castle.

"Nonnegotiable," Mallet confirmed. "It's right there in the Iron Teen contract. Didn't you read the fine print, my dear?"

"I—I thought you didn't take recruits until after the finals," she stammered.

Mallet sidled up to her. "You understand that a refusal will result in forfeiture of all your winnings," she said. "And it will trigger an investigation. Why would anyone not want this prestigious honor?"

Under the pressure of Mallet's gaze, Robyn weighed her options. She did not want to agree to join the Military Police, even as a cover. The very thought was laughable.

Robyn steeled herself for what was necessary. *Eye on the prize*, she reminded herself. She would get to go to Castle District, to the governor's mansion, and if she made it that far, nothing could stop her from finding her mother in the dungeon. Find her. Then free her.

"You really think I'm cut out to be an MP?" Robyn mused, channeling as much enthusiasm as she could into her voice. "That's amazing."

With the cordon of MPs tightening behind her, Robyn had a feeling that they wouldn't let her leave. They might ship her straight to the place right now.

Mallet's cold smile turned icy. "I was being polite," she said. "Allowing you a chance to come to the right decision on your own. But even the most reluctant inductees find a true home at the academy, in time. Isn't that right, MP Mullin?"

Jeb snapped to attention. "It's a privilege to serve, ma'am."

He met Robyn's gaze. Behind his firm, very cop-like stare, Robyn read soft strobes of desperation. There was no other choice, she realized. No way off this stage. Crowd at her knees. MPs at her back. Mallet might as well have placed her hand at Robyn's throat.

Become an MP willingly, or be taken by force, investigated, and probably imprisoned. Robyn knew she had had no choice. She clung to the glimmer of hope that, despite her first reaction, she could convince Mallet that she wanted to be an MP. That she would behave and fall in line. If she could hold out long enough to make it to the governor's dinner, all would not be lost.

"It would indeed be a privilege to serve," Robyn echoed. "Thank you for this opportunity."

"Please join me onstage," Sheriff Mallet said. "And formally accept your post."

"Iron Teen winner is Roberta Calzone." Cheers went up from the crowd.

It had been her intention to arrest the hoodlum on the spot. In front of the crowds. Let the people of Sherwood know once and for all who was in charge. To let them know their beloved outlaw's reign was over.

But the cheers going up for the girl stalled her.

Sherwoodians loved their Iron Teen winners. Time had proven this. Year after year, the energy swelled and grew from the preliminary round through to the finals. Thousands upon thousands were prepared to rally behind this one girl.

It was too much power.

Mallet prided herself on strategy. Arresting the girl would be a mistake. To tell a crowd that was primed to love Roberta Calzone as their Iron Teen winner that the very same girl was the one wreaking havoc on Sherwood?

Sheriff Mallet's fluttering gut screamed: *recipe for disaster*. She would be handing the hoodlum a platform, handing her followers she didn't earn and didn't deserve.

No. It would be better to handle this quietly.

During the ceremony, Robyn looked out over the crowd. Her eye fell on a gruff-looking man. Chazz! What was he doing here? He rarely left T.C. Chazz wore an expression Robyn had never seen on him. It reminded her of her father right then, how he often looked during her gymnastics meets back home. The mixed expression of pride and concern on Chazz's face matched one of Dad's very closely. Robyn felt a now-familiar twinge of sorrow. How amazed and proud would her parents be if they could see her now, with a gold medal around her neck?

The people had flowed out of the bleachers and were now filling the field beneath her. Seeing Chazz reminded her of how good it felt to help people. She remembered what the moon lore had promised about her being special. The many faces spoke of her father's determination to help Sherwood through his work in Parliament. The work Robyn now continued, in her outlaw ways.

She felt guilty. How could she for one second even pretend that she'd join the ranks of the people who killed or imprisoned him and imprisoned her mom. As badly as she wanted to find her mom, it was a betrayal to stand in front of the crowd and pretend to be okay with the MPs. Robyn grew more and more sure of it as she stood there. She needed a better plan.

≪CHAPTER THIRTY≫

Conscripted!

"What's going on?" Key demanded, shattering the afternoon quiet of the cathedral.

Scarlet shook her head, confused. "They weren't supposed to take them all into custody," Scarlet said. "That's not normal. Something must've happened."

"Do you think they're onto her?"

"They can't be," Scarlet said. "Mallet had a whole crowd of Sherwoodians right there. If she knew she had Robyn in custody, she would've been grandstanding for hours."

"Maybe," Jeb countered. "The top MPs have been sniffing around something. Mallet's got them all on edge." He added, "I got the temporary Tag back on her, but, if it's smudged . . ."

Scarlet paced. "The smallest glitch could expose her."

"Last year, they didn't conscript us until after finals. We got to go home."

"That's what was supposed to happen." Scarlet showed them a printed page. It was a checkpoint pass, for traveling from Sherwood to Castle District. With the name Roberta Calzone typed in small letters in the top right corner. "I took this from the registration tent. They started printing them up as soon as the contest was over."

"That's not good," Key said. "It means holding the winners was a last-minute change."

Scarlet nodded agreement. "The only good thing is that we have the pass now," she said. "We can use it to get into Castle and go through with the prison break."

"Without Robyn?" Laurel piped up.

"With or without her," Scarlet said. "Remember, she's got her own ride into Castle District now."

Jeb sighed. "Assuming she's still just a contestant and they haven't thrown her in prison herself."

"Can't you find out?" Laurel asked, tucking herself small.

"Maybe," Jeb says. "But I think we'd already know. Mallet would announce it to the world the minute Robyn was caught."

"It feels wrong," Key muttered. He thumped his fist into his other palm. "Why did she have to go and do this?"

"You couldn't have stopped her," Laurel said. "She wanted it real bad."

"She went behind my back," Key thundered. "Behind all of our backs!" He glared at Scarlet and Jeb. "Well, not *all* of our backs, it sounds like."

"She didn't think you'd agree with her choice," Scarlet snapped. "And it wasn't worth the fight. She didn't even know if she stood a chance of making the top six."

Key threw up his hands. "I'm so tired of this fight. I don't know why we even bother."

"You have no idea what it means to put yourself on the line like she has," Scarlet retorted. "Stop judging her."

"If you think—" Key started.

"Stop it!" Laurel shrieked, popping her fingers into her ears. "Stop yelling." Her round brown eyes shimmered. "Robyn's in big trouble."

The room echoed into silence.

"We can't help her now," Key said softly. "We don't know where she is."

"And there's a chance they know she's Robyn?" Laurel asked, tears spilling over.

"A chance," Jeb said.

"Then we *can* help her." Laurel's expression turned determined. "We can make sure they're still looking for Robyn." She held up a small green pad of sticky notes.

After a moment, Key understood what she meant. "Remind them that the rebellion is bigger than one girl."

"And make them question whether they've actually got her," Jeb said.

They huddled in silence for a minute. It wouldn't do to argue any more. What was done was done. Wherever Robyn was, she was out of reach. But the Robyn Hoodlum mission could go on.

"Merryan's coming in an hour with the final plans," Scarlet said. "Anyone who wants to help, be here." She stalked away from them.

The MPs whisked Robyn and the other finalists into jeeps and rushed them to the MP trainee barracks. Her accommodation for the night was a spare, single room, with a low cot and a water spigot. If this was how MP trainees lived, it was a wonder that anyone ever joined up. Robyn looked out the narrow window at endless grassy fields, wondering if she was still in Sherwood.

The door creaked. Mallet entered.

"This was the only private space available for the moment, and I wanted to have a little chat," the sheriff said.

"Okay," Robyn said, unsure what to make of the situation.

"You looked familiar to me." Mallet clasped her hands behind her back and paced the room. "I actually thought"—she laughed lightly, in self-deprecation—"that you might be Robyn."

"Robyn?" Robyn echoed. "Me? Really?" She hoped the puzzled tone was convincing.

"Hmm. But then the hoodlum struck again tonight," Mallet continued. "So clearly it is not you."

"Of course not," Robyn agreed. "What would that hoodlum want with Iron Teen? Surely there are better ways to acquire Points?" She forced herself to laugh.

"Surely." Mallet reached out suddenly and took hold of Robyn's pendant. "What an interesting trinket," she said.

Robyn's heart deflated. The jig was up. Mallet knew perfectly well where she'd seen that necklace before. Her too-casual tone made that clear.

"Unfortunately, contestants aren't allowed to wear any jewelry. For safety."

The sheriff slid the pendant pair around her own neck. Robyn fought the urge to leap up and snatch it back. "I'll need it returned afterward," she said. "It's very special to me."

"I'll keep it safe," the sheriff promised. "And in exchange, you'll go through with the contest and cause me no trouble."

"Why wouldn't I?" Robyn asked, but she was confused. What was Mallet playing at?

"You will go through with this contest," Mallet repeated. "And you will find a way to call off your friends. The reign of the hoodlum Robyn ends tonight."

Fat chance, Robyn thought. "What's in it for me?"

"A long life in prison," Mallet offered. "As opposed to a swift execution." The people of Sherwood loved their Iron Teen winners. They also loved their resident hoodlum. A marriage of two such hero figures might lead to full-scale rebellion.

"If I announce your capture now, while these thefts continue, it will look like I don't have control of my city."

"Appearances?" Robyn said.

The sheriff's smile spread like ice across a placid lake. "Make no mistake. I am always in control."

"You underestimate me," Robyn said, steam heat in her belly.

"And you me," Mallet retorted. "I didn't even have to catch you. You walked right in."

"Maybe that was part of my plan."

A flicker of uncertainty flashed in the sheriff's eyes. The girl's threats were of no consequence. The governor would be informed that the hoodlum had been captured. He would easily be convinced that it was best for all concerned if no announcement was made. The girl known as Robyn Hoodlum would simply disappear.

"They'll take you to your room now," Mallet said.

⪡CHAPTER THIRTY-ONE⪢

Masquerade

In the morning, Tucker drove the borrowed van toward the checkpoint with Scarlet in the passenger seat. She held Roberta Calzone's pass to go to Castle District. The others hid in the back, concealed behind carved-out metal tool chests.

"Let's just hope the border guards didn't get the memo about the contestants being detained already," Scarlet said.

"From your lips," Tucker muttered as they pulled up to the Sherwood exit checkpoint. He rolled down the window to greet the guards.

"This is my niece Roberta. She's a finalist in the Iron Teen contest!" Tucker blurted. "I'm taking her down to compete! We've never been to Castle District. We have a pass today!"

Tucker thrust the paperwork out the window. The MP took it and looked at it carefully.

"She came in first place in the Sherwood competition, isn't that something? First place. Only six kids get to go, you know. She's really something, our Roberta."

Scarlet smiled brightly. Then she tried to school her features into an obedient, MP-ready expression.

The MP's gaze flicked over her then returned to focus on Tucker. He handed back the paperwork. It was actually legitimate, after all, Scarlet reminded herself. There shouldn't be a problem, unless—

"We'll need to open your rear," the MP said.

Scarlet's heart sank like a two-ton rock.

"Sure, yeah, sure," Tucker said. He carried on the part of eager innocent quite well.

"Can I come out and open it?" he asked. "The door sticks a bit, you've got to jimmy it with your shoulder." He made a frantic twitching motion that, in other circumstances, would have caused Scarlet to burst out laughing. But the weight of the dire moment overrode all humor.

Tucker slid out of the van and made his way around. "Excuse the mess," he said. "I've never crossed out of Sherwood since the checkpoints went up. This is a special occasion, you know; my niece is an Iron Teen finalist. I'm a local guy myself . . ."

Loud thumping shook the van all the way up to the cab. "I didn't know how this would go," Tucker rambled good-naturedly. Scarlet picked up the conversation again as the rear doors swung open. "It's my work truck, you see. Only one in the family with a car, and it's the only one I've got. If you need me to empty it all, that's going to take awhile."

Scarlet prepared herself to leap into the driver's seat and gun it.

"That won't be necessary," the MP said. "Good luck to the kid, okay?"

"Yeah, yeah, sure. Thanks. She's talented. First place, you know. Out of hundreds!"

"Right," the MP said. "You can go on now. Thanks."

"I'll let you all know how she does on the way back through. She's a winner, I know that much already!"

The MP rolled his eyes behind Tucker's back. "We'll look forward to it. Have a good day."

Scarlet held back a snicker. Now that the moment of maximum danger had passed, it was easier to appreciate Tucker's comedy routine.

He jumped into the cab and proclaimed "Castle District, ho!" for the benefit of the MPs.

As soon as his window rolled all the way up and the van left, Scarlet dissolved into laughter. "Thanks, Unc. Not proud of me at all there, are ya?"

Tucker's cheesy grin faded into a sigh. "I don't think I've ever been so scared in my life."

"Wouldn't know it to look at you," she said. "You faked it well."

Tucker lifted one hand off the steering wheel. It was trembling. "Here's hoping that the hardest part is behind us."

Scarlet nodded. It was a nice thought. But gazing through the windshield at the golden dome of the governor's mansion she knew the truth: the hard part had barely begun.

≪CHAPTER THIRTY-TWO≫

Promises

The MP jeeps carried Robyn and the other contestants straight through the city center in a swift convoy that barely stopped for red lights. Robyn stared up at the governor's mansion as they drove down the wide, tree-lined boulevard leading up to it.

Keep silent, and take the fall? Betray her team and reveal herself as the hoodlum? Robyn shook her head at the predicament. It was going to be fine. It had to be. She'd get away somehow.

They climbed a mountain of marble steps to enter the governor's mansion. Escape was not an option. Anyway, Robyn barely gave it a thought. She had made it.

Iron Teen officials waited in the vaulted atrium. The ceiling yawned upward like the back of a throat, a massive chandelier dangling like a uvula overhead. All the air seemed to be sucked out of the space. Robyn found herself struggling to breathe.

"You nervous, honey?" a tall MP beside her said in a condescending voice.

"Never," she lied. "I've got this."

Robyn pasted a smile on her face and marched up to the Iron Teen MPs. They had a name badge and a folder of information for her. From the folder they pulled contract after contract.

"That's a lot of paperwork." Robyn signed each sheet "Roberta Calzone." The MPs asked no questions. They handed her an orange T-shirt with 'Sherwood' written on it in large block letters, front and back. Then simply led her toward the room where the contestants were to gather.

It was a large conference room, with a long table ringed with cushy executive chairs. A whiteboard on one end of the room reflected a holographic projection of the Iron Teen contest logo.

There were a handful of other contestants in the room. They sat solo in chairs or stood around the snack cart chatting. Folded T-shirts that represented their counties were strewn about the room.

Robyn barely looked at them. She sat in a chair, leaned back against the hinges, and closed her eyes. She forced herself to sit as still as possible and tried to calm her breathing. Motionlessness. It required all the energy she had not to race out of the room and start tearing through the halls.

Somewhere, several stories below, Robyn's mother waited in a cold, damp cell. Never knowing her daughter was so close or that she was coming to save her.

Four stories directly above Robyn, Sheriff Marissa Mallet strode down the marbled hallway toward the governor's private office. She did not enjoy being summoned to Crown's chambers, but she supposed it was better than being ignored.

And today, at last, she had a piece of good news to share. This meeting would not be in vain. Mallet was determined to resecure the promotion Crown had promised her for spearheading the rebel "disappearances" several months ago.

She stepped into Crown's outer office. Bill Pillsbury, the governor's press secretary, stood in the entryway talking with Crown's assistant. He looked up from the conversation as the sheriff entered.

"Marissa."

"Pill."

"Have you got the Iron Teen group photo yet? I need it within the hour if it's to go up on the news tonight."

"The contestants have all arrived. The volunteers are staging the photo now. You'll have it."

"Very well." Pillsbury stalked off toward his office, offering a flick of a wave to the governor's assistant. *What a jerk*, Mallet thought. At least he didn't waste words.

Mallet looked through the set of double doors toward the chief of staff's bullpen. The crew of young staffers appeared hard at work.

"Shiffley here?" Mallet asked the assistant.

"In the governor's office, Sheriff. They're expecting you."

Mallet tamped down the surge of annoyance. She'd hoped to have a moment alone with the governor, lest Shiffley find a way to take credit for her efforts. "Thanks."

The sheriff straightened her jacket and strode calmly into the governor's chambers.

"Come to play games, Sheriff?" Crown said the moment she stepped onto the carpet. "You must have plenty of time on your hands."

Shiffley chuckled coldly, seated in one of the two armchairs facing Crown's desk.

Mallet swallowed the subtle reprimand, as she knew she was supposed to. She chose not to slide into the matching chair, but placed her hand along its back and remained standing. "Sir, the contest is our prime recruiting ground. Catching Robyn remains the priority of the day, but funneling their strongest into our training program has important long-term implications."

"Understood, Sheriff," Shiffley said.

"Your innovation in that area has been noted," Crown commented. "Moving on."

Mallet nodded. "Yes, sir. There's one particularly interesting candidate this year, a young woman—"

Crown waved his hand, uninterested. "Dismissed."

"One moment, please, sir," Mallet objected. "I haven't told you the good news yet."

"What is it?" Crown demanded.

"My lab has uncoded a piece of DNA evidence the hoodlum left at a crime scene."

"Oh?"

"They are running the match now. I've instructed them to message me the results immediately." The results would be altered, of course, to confirm a match to Roberta Calzone. The lab tech would be dealt with as needed.

Crown narrowed his eyes and tapped his mustache. "Excellent. That means—"

"Within the next few hours, we'll know the true identity of the girl who calls herself Robyn. I expect to have her in custody by nightfall."

≪CHAPTER THIRTY-THREE≫

Winners' Dinner

In the contestants' room, Robyn started to get the lay of the land. She gravitated toward the other Sherwood winners, whom she recognized. Speedy was among them. It turned out his real name was Karl, but Robyn couldn't shake the nickname in her mind. The other finalists were three boys and a girl. She had a short, stocky gymnast's build. Basically the opposite of Robyn's lean, lanky physique. They eyed each other warily.

There seemed to be a hint of solidarity, but at the same time everyone knew they couldn't become friends or allies. They'd be competing together again soon enough. Robyn tried to act like she still cared about the contest, but her mind was already someplace six stories below.

Mallet strode into the room and everyone fell quiet. The volunteers, including Merryan, separated like water after a drop of oil. They spread out against the walls leaving Mallet alone at the front of the room. The white wall behind her dimmed to a grayish red.

Robyn blinked, thinking she had imagined the ominous color shift. She hadn't. There were screen corners at the edge of the wall, which projected the Iron Teen logo. A video clip began playing. It was the same Iron Teen TV ad Robyn remembered seeing many times back home in Castle. She used to sing along to the theme music and leap around the living room in echoes of what was happening on-screen.

"You've all aspired to greatness and performed well under pressure," Mallet said as the video wound down. "Congratulations."

This was an obvious sales pitch for the MP training program. They wanted people to join voluntarily. Even though it was mandatory, Robyn realized, the people around the table might not all still realize that. Who knew what the winners from the other counties had been told? Robyn wondered in particular if the winners from Castle District had any idea about the conscription—or if they would even be pulled in unless they wanted to be. Crown had to keep up appearances in Castle, after all.

Robyn shivered. She wanted to make waves about it, to call attention to the hypocrisy, but she couldn't afford to draw attention to herself. She didn't want to do anything that might result in increased scrutiny by the powers that be.

She sat quietly and listened as Mallet gave a spiel about serving the people. Robyn knew all about serving the people. She calmly met the sheriff's eyes as she gazed around the table at each "recruit" in turn.

When the meeting wound down, the contestants got up and prepared to head to the dining room.

"Roberta," Mallet said in a tone that bordered on warmth. "Nice to see you doing well here." The veiled message was clearly meant to remind her of her obligations.

"Thanks, Sheriff," she answered, taking the woman's outstretched hand. "You have no idea how much it means to me to be here."

It felt strange still, moving through the world without gloves on. Scarlet's fake Tag remained Robyn's only protection from the discovery of her true identity. At least tonight she didn't have to worry about weather messing with her plans.

See that she doesn't wash. The sheriff's words to the guard outside her cell floated back to Robyn. Mallet had inspected her fake Tag, too. She wanted it to remain in place for some reason? Why? If Roberta Calzone was revealed as Robyn Loxley, what would it matter to the sheriff?

Through the sheriff's white button-down shirt, she could see the faint outline of the sun-moon keys. Why was the sheriff still wearing her pendant? Did she have any idea of the significance of the artifact?

"Good luck tomorrow." Mallet withdrew her hand.

Robyn smiled. She'd take the luck. But it wasn't tomorrow she'd need it. It was tonight.

The twenty finalists filed into the long dining room. It was less ornate than Robyn was expecting. She remembered being in this room once, long ago. The sconces had seemed so high and golden and the tables so huge and long. She had been much smaller then, and more easily dazzled. Now the magic of the space had utterly vanished, eclipsed by the knowledge that somewhere in the lower floors of this building her mother was being held captive.

Robyn found her place card and sat down.

When Crown walked in, the whole room suddenly stilled, as if a thin layer of ice had been cast over everything. The chandeliers stopped swaying lightly in the breeze from movement below. The china place settings quivered and then fell still. When he spoke, the air itself became colder.

"Good evening."

"Good evening," the whole room chorused in response.

Crown smiled. "Welcome to the Iron Teen winners'

dinner. It's a pleasure to welcome such fine athletes into my home and into the heart of our new city."

Robyn fought the urge to gag. Who did Crown think he was? Oh, right—the dictator who had "won" the hearts of the city.

As he invited the diners to take a seat, Robyn clenched her fists beneath the table.

Waiters came through with steaming platters of delicious-smelling food. The other contestants dove into the meal with the vigor they'd taken to the obstacle course. Robyn spooned a few items onto her plate so it wouldn't be conspicuously empty. She could only hope there'd be something left for her to enjoy when she returned.

"I need to use the ladies' room," she whispered to the chaperone seated nearest her.

The woman dabbed her lips with her napkin and pushed back from the table. "I'll show you the way."

Uh-oh. "I can find it," Robyn said quickly.

The woman led her out of the dining room and down a long hallway. Was the woman going to stand there and wait for Robyn to finish? She hadn't been expecting a chaperone. That would give her very little time before she was missed and checked on.

"The food smelled great, didn't it?" Robyn said casually. "I'll hurry back so I can enjoy it. I can find my way back," she added, when the woman made no move to leave her. She pointed toward the dining room. "I have a very good sense of direction."

"Nonsense," said the chaperone, perhaps a little too lightly. "I'll wait."

"Thank you," Robyn said politely. She pushed open the rest room door and crossed into the sitting room, where Merryan was waiting.

≪CHAPTER THIRTY-FOUR≫

Into the Dungeon

"Oh, thank the moon," Merryan gushed, rushing toward her. "You made it. Are you okay?" She threw her soft arms tight around Robyn.

"Well, I'm here, aren't I?" Robyn's tone came out a little sharper than she'd meant it to. Nerves and frustration overflowing. There was no time for comfort. Only action.

Merryan's face drooped as she pulled away. "Okay. Sorry."

"No, *I'm* sorry." Robyn felt bad for snapping at her friend, who was only trying to help. She didn't deserve to be yelled at. Merryan put a hand on Robyn's shoulder.

"I'm a little freaked out," Robyn admitted. "House arrest was unexpected."

"I didn't think you ever got scared," Merryan said. "Meanwhile I'm a whole puddle of nerves over here." She handed Robyn her disguise.

Robyn quickly changed from her colorful Iron Teen outfit to her hoodlum-wear. Black leggings, black T-shirt, and the red beret with her braid sewn into it. If any guards or security cameras did happen to catch sight of her tearing through the hallways, she wouldn't blow her cover completely.

"I have a chaperone," Robyn warned.

"We'll go out the other way." Merryan indicated a second exit from the bathroom.

"More like a guard," Robyn amended. "Mallet knows."

Merryan's eyes rounded. "She knows that you're Robyn? How?"

"Recognized me, I guess. She knows everything."

"Why aren't you under arrest?"

"Still trying to figure that out," Robyn answered. "She has some kind of agenda." She studied the slant of her beret in the mirror.

"Are you ready?" Merryan asked.

"Let's go." They pushed open the opposite door. Robyn wondered how long would pass before the chaperone would miss her and come looking. Hopefully no earnest search would begin until she was long gone with Mom and the other prisoners in tow.

The corridor was long and quiet. Too quiet. No sign of guards or workers. A slight clanking noise, like a ticking pipe, was all Robyn heard. It was almost creepy, she thought as she tiptoed along.

"Is it totally weird, living here?"

"I'm used to it now," Merryan replied. There were layers of sadness in her voice.

The marble halls echoed eerily with their small footsteps.

"Why are there no guards here?" Robyn asked.

"Most of the mansion is unguarded," Merryan answered. "It's only the cameras, because the hard part would be actually getting in here in the first place."

"Right. Smile for the cameras."

"They're watching, but they mostly ignore me. I'm allowed to move about this part of the mansion freely. And anyway, I've been having friends come over a lot lately. They're used to seeing me with another girl."

Merryan was even more clever than Robyn had given her credit for.

"I always give them a bit of a tour, too," Merryan said. "So the guards probably won't think anything of it."

Robyn smiled. Yeah, Merryan was miles smarter than any of Robyn's old classmates from Castle. "We should've been friends before," Robyn said.

Merryan smiled. "I always thought so. You're the one who wanted to be off on your own all the time."

"I guess I wasn't looking in the right places," Robyn said. "You seemed like you liked the popular crowd. All that girly stuff."

"Nah." Merryan shrugged. "I spent too much time acting the way I thought I was supposed to. You always did your own thing. That's way cool to me. Brave."

"You're brave," Robyn said. "Obviously."

Merryan grinned. "Only since I started hanging out with you." Her smile faded as they crossed through a small, plant-filled atrium. "This is where it gets dicey." She placed a hand on Robyn's arm as they strolled toward the first round of security. "Come in here."

The girls ducked behind a huge flowering bush. Long fernlike leaves sprouted from a pot the height of Robyn's chest. It was big enough around to conceal them both from the pair of guards that passed moments later.

"The guards walk the floor every thirty minutes." Merryan checked her watch. "It's almost time for the shift change."

Robyn could clearly see Merryan's long-term effort. She chided herself for the impatience she'd shown her in the past few weeks. Clearly Merryan had been working hard for the team all along. The mansion was truly enormous.

"Thanks for doing this," Robyn told her.

"Yeah."

"It must be weird, going against your uncle."

"I don't think of it like that," Merryan said. "I'm not hurting him. I'm stopping him from hurting others."

"That's true," Robyn said.

It was brave what Merryan was doing, but when push came to shove, where would her loyalties lie? Robyn wasn't sure she'd be able to go against her own family, even if they were bad. Maybe Merryan was the bravest one of them all.

"Come on," Merryan said. "It's time."

"You sneak down like this every time?"

Merryan shrugged. "They look the other way when I go down to the dungeons, I guess. No one has said anything to me about it."

"But we can't assume they'll be okay with you bringing a friend."

"Right," Merryan said. "That's why we have this." She pulled out her copy of the hand-drawn map of hallway cameras for the dungeon area.

Merryan's drawing, improved for appearances by Key, was pretty accurate so far. As she peeked around the next corner, Robyn glanced up to see the camera mounted exactly where Merryan described.

Somewhere else in the building, Scarlet would be holed up, wreaking havoc on Crown's security. Robyn could only hope that it all happened on schedule.

"I'll go get the others," Merryan said. "Wait here, and make sure the guards pass before I get back."

"Okay," Robyn said.

The last stretch of hallway appeared completely empty. Robyn wasn't taking any chances. She lingered in the adjoining hall and held her breath. In the center of the next corridor, the old-fashioned barred door was fitted with a new computerized combination padlock. The guards' footsteps echoed in the hall. Robyn pulled back and waited until the sound receded.

Merryan returned a few minutes later with Scarlet and Key.

"Where's Laurel?" whispered Robyn.

"With Tucker," Key answered. "Preparing our exit."

"Now or never," Merryan informed them, checking her watch. "You're sure the cameras in this sector are out?"

"On a loop," Scarlet assured them. "Until I take it off. Or the battery runs out. They were looking a little low, come to think."

Key glowered. "Not funny."

Scarlet grinned. "Just a little break-in humor."

No one else laughed.

"Wow. Tough room." Scarlet lifted her keypad. "Let's get this show on the road, eh?"

≪CHAPTER THIRTY-FIVE≫

Anonymous Rescue

The corridor leading into the dungeon was dank and humid. It smelled like mildew and sweat, like the locker room at an indoor pool. There was no water anywhere that Robyn could see, but it must've been someplace. A single row of tubular lightbulbs snaked down the center of the ceiling, painting the corridor in pale grayish light. The floor sloped downward and curved sharply out of sight.

"It's not far," Merryan said. "Hurry. We only have a few minutes."

"Until what?" Robyn asked.

"Until the guards come by."

"I thought the dungeon wasn't guarded," Scarlet said.

"It's not. They do rounds, though."

"During the shift change?" Robyn said.

"Before it and after it."

"And we're breaking in now?" Scarlet muttered.

Robyn suddenly wished she'd paid more attention to the details of the plan.

"Trust me," Merryan said. "I've been over the timing. Alone and with Key. This is the only way."

The corridor ended suddenly, at a large earthen door.

"We're here."

"Way to state the obvious, Castle," Scarlet murmured.

The door creaked open, and the team of outlaws plunged deeper into the dungeon.

The dim, cave-like space was lined with bars on the inside, too. A ring-shaped enclosure separated the small foyer where Robyn stood from the cell. The floor was packed dirt, the walls old stone. A few sconces mounted on either side of the door lit the room enough to see.

Behind the bars a collection of women crouched, or sat, or lay, in small clusters together.

"Mom?" Robyn blurted out.

"Robyn?" a woman's voice. "By the moon, what are you doing here?" A shadowy figure crawled toward the bars.

"Mom!" Robyn dropped to her knees and stuck her arms through the bars, grasping for her mother's wrists.

"Oh, honey. It is you." Mrs. Loxley petted Robyn's cheek. "How is this possible?"

"You wouldn't believe me if I told you," Robyn whispered. She closed her eyes. The familiar cup of Mom's palm against her cheek took her away from this place, to somewhere safe and warm and long ago.

Scarlet was already at work on the digital keypad barring the door. Her fingers flew over the tablet surface. When it clicked free, she moved onto the next. Key and Merryan levered the doors open.

"No time for chitchat," Key said. "We gotta get them out of here."

"We only have a few minutes," Merryan said.

"What?" said Mrs. Loxley. "What are you talking about?"

Robyn darted into the cell and pulled her mom to her feet. Proudly, she announced, "We're here to free you."

"Unbelievable!" Shiffley roared from behind his thick wooden office door. His outrage permeated the walls. The three young staffers slaving at their cubicles jumped, then froze as their boss slammed into the room.

"Find Sheriff Mallet. I want to know the meaning of this," he ordered, thumping past them all, headed for the governor's office suite.

Bill Pillsbury poked his head in through the doorway. "Good heavens," he uttered calmly. "Whatever is going on?"

"Intruder alert," said Rossman, straightening his perfectly straight tie.

"Dungeon keypad alarm," added Clark. "Possible prison break?"

"Very good, then," Pill said, his eyebrows knitting themselves into a V. "We're bound to have news to report at eleven." He disappeared as quickly as he'd appeared.

Robyn left her traditional note, pierced with string and tied to the bars of the now-empty cell. Scarlet was already headed out the tunnel exit, scoping their path. Merryan followed, taking the arm of one of the women. They were frail, after months of hunger, and stiff from the crouched stillness of confinement. They blinked and stumbled, helping each other along. Key took up the back of the procession, aiding the slowest.

Robyn didn't want to let go of her mom, but so many of the women were weaker. Mrs. Loxley gently shrugged out of her daughter's grasp. "Let me help them," she said. "We'll be together again soon."

Scarlet let out a small yelp. A commotion ensued at the first door.

"Guards!" Merryan whispered, holding up a hand to stop the others. Then she raced up to join Scarlet.

All Robyn could hear was the governor's niece

scrambling through some sort of explanation. Robyn tucked her braid tail up inside her beret and stepped into the hall to join them. She pushed the dungeon's wooden door shut behind her. A pair of guards loomed over the girls, looking menacing in their muscles and uniforms.

"This area is off-limits, Miss Crown," one guard said. "What do you think you're doing?"

"It was wrong of me, I know," Merryan babbled. "I accidentally told my friends about the dungeon, and they didn't believe it was real. Obviously we didn't go all the way in . . . There's nothing to worry about. We'll just—" She started to walk away.

"I don't think so, Miss Crown." The guard crossed his arms. "We've had reports of intruders in the building. I'm afraid I'll have to detain your friends for questioning."

Robyn swallowed hard. Scarlet looked like she was about to bolt.

"Is that really necessary?" Merryan rambled on. The girl managed to sound clueless, innocent, and awkward, and she seemed so very natural about it.

A man in a suit raced into the hallway behind the two guards. He pulled up short when he saw the group standing there. He composed himself and strode toward them.

"Look here," he barked. "What's going on down here?"

Robyn recognized him as he came closer. Bill Pillsbury, a colleague of her father's. He had run the press office for Parliament. If he wasn't among the disappeared, it meant he had taken Crown's side. Robyn narrowed her eyes. Traitor.

"Merryan, dear. There you are. I've been looking everywhere. Officers, you're aware that this is the governor's niece?"

The MPs turned to face him, putting their backs to the girls. "Yes, sir. We were sent to check on the pris—"

The second MP coughed loudly. And fakely. "To check on this sector," he said, loud enough to cover the voice of his cohort. "We're on an intruder alert."

"Yes, yes." Pillsbury waved one arm wildly. "Leave the children with me and get on with it."

In the course of his arm waving, Pillsbury flicked his jacket aside. It was a weird, unnatural movement, Robyn thought. A muscle spasm, or something. Her gaze followed the motion automatically. His fingers drifted over the black gadget clipped to his belt. An old-style TexTer, like her father's!

Robyn yanked her attention upward. Her eyes met Pillsbury's. He nodded succinctly.

He released his hand and his jacket covered up the device again.

He was the one! The anonymous person who'd been texting her all this time. With warnings.

Robyn didn't know what game Pillsbury might be playing here. No time to dwell on it now. He had created enough of a distraction that she could escape with her friends.

"Gentlemen," Pillsbury barked. "Don't tell me it is your habit to interrogate the niece of the governor and her friends?"

"Sir, no."

"Look at me!" Pillsbury's low, gravelly voice commanded attention. The MPs snapped around to face him again. He advanced on them, broad-shouldered and intimidating.

"I report directly to Crown, which means you report to me. The two of you are so many levels below me I don't even know how to count them."

Pillsbury's voice rose, and his hand, down at his side, subtly beckoned the children to continue the exodus.

Robyn eased the door open, just enough to allow the others to pass.

The prisoners tiptoed past, the stronger ones supporting the weaker ones. Key alone took the lead, because Robyn, Merryan, and Scarlet had to stay near the guards. They couldn't very well disappear.

"Sir, they're not supposed to be down here."

"They're only children. Children misbehave. No harm, no foul. Do you have children, officers?"

They shook their heads.

"Ah," Pillsbury said. "Then you probably think punishment from MPs is worse than what discipline a parent can hand down."

"Well, we have parents, sir."

"Quite right. The girl is in her own home. Her guardian should be the one to handle this." Pillsbury paused. "Unless—would you like to be the ones to bring her up to the governor's office?"

The MPs glanced at each other. "Sir, our protocol would be to retain the intruders in the MP offices."

"Intruders?" Pillsbury shook his head. "Merryan and her friends will go upstairs and apologize to her uncle for breaking the mansion rules. I will make sure that happens."

⊰CHAPTER THIRTY-SIX⊱

For Sherwood, Unite

Pillsbury hurried with the girls through the halls toward Merryan's scouted exit route.

"You've a plan to get the prisoners out?" he said.

"Yes," Robyn assured him.

"Very well. I'll be in touch." He left them at a corner and disappeared in the opposite direction.

"Who *was* that?" Scarlet said. "He was awesome. And freaky as all get-out."

"I'll explain later," Robyn promised.

Merryan led them to the second-floor room where Key was helping the last of the prisoners climb out the window. None of the unguarded first-floor rooms had windows, unfortunately.

The rope ladder down one story was slow going for the weakest ones, but they wanted freedom badly enough to take the pain. At the bottom of the ladder, Laurel was helping the women ease down. Tucker hustled them away, a few at a time, through the land-scaped gardens, toward the high fence at the back of the property.

Key started to climb down himself. Scarlet went next. Robyn prepared to follow. But instead she turned back and threw her arms around Merryan. "Thank you."

If it wasn't for her, Mom would still be trapped, possibly forever.

"It's no problem," Merryan said. But she was wrong about that, and they both knew it. What she had done was about to cause big problems for Merryan.

"You could come," Robyn whispered. "We can take care of you."

Merryan shook her head. "Someone has to stay," she said. "And explain to my uncle."

Robyn climbed onto the ladder. It was hard to leave her. "You'll be in big trouble."

"I'll take the blame. It'll be okay."

"But—"

"Go," Merryan urged. "They need you."

"We need you, too." Robyn leaned back through the window and kissed Merryan on the cheek.

Merryan's face flushed. "I'll be fine," she promised. "Uncle Iggy won't hurt me."

That seemed optimistic.

"It's not really my fault, you know." Merryan said, twirling a lock of her hair and putting on a blank, innocent expression. "I'm just one little girl."

Merryan could handle herself, sure enough. Robyn grinned as she climbed down and raced through the mansion gardens, winding among thick-scented flowers and decorative sculpted bushes. The escape plan was going as well as could be expected. She could safely leave the Iron Teen contest in her dust. A tiny burst of excitement snuck into her. She couldn't wait to tell Mom that she had competed, and won!

The fence consisted of slender iron bars spaced about eight inches apart. Tucker and Laurel had used a carjack to bend apart two of the bars, levering open a gap wide enough for people to pass through. Scarlet and Laurel were slipping through now.

At the other side of the fence, Tucker had pulled the van close, and they loaded the women into the back of it. Key and Mrs. Loxley helped her friends climb in and get situated. It would surely be a tight fit for all eighteen of them, but it was only temporary.

By the time Robyn approached the fence, only two more women had to climb in, plus Mrs. Loxley and the rest of Robyn's crew.

A quartet of MPs barreled around the corner, guns drawn. They emerged with no warning—the garden foliage had concealed their approach. The guards spread into a half circle, trapping the van and its would-be passengers against the fence. Key spun around, as if looking for an exit. The MPs had them surrounded.

≪CHAPTER THIRTY-SEVEN≫

For Sherwood, We Fight

The women didn't hesitate. The three who were not yet in the van barely glanced at each other before acting. They split in three directions, each diving toward one of the MPs.

"No!" Robyn raced across the grass. "Mom!"

A gun went off, in one of the struggles. Robyn could not tell where. She slithered through the gap in the fence bars, but it was too late. The women, including Mrs. Loxley, wrestled with the MPs. They had caught the guards by surprise by jumping on them, but now were quickly being subdued.

"Robyn," her mother choked out, "Get the others out of here!"

The fourth MP hurried to the front of the van, where Tucker was scrambling to start the engine. He reached in the open window and grasped Tucker by the throat.

Tucker punched at him, but the MP dodged his attack and dragged Tucker free of the vehicle.

The driver's door stood open, very close to the fence gap.

"Mom!" Robyn cried again. There was no way she was going to leave her behind.

"Go!" Mrs. Loxley shouted. "First for the rebellion!"

No one gets left behind. Robyn lunged forward and kicked the guard holding Tucker in the . . . sensitive place. He doubled over. Tucker broke free, but didn't return to the van. Instead he wrapped his arms around the MP and tackled him to the ground.

"Take them away," he shouted to Robyn. The ignition was running.

Shots rang out again from one of the MPs who had been distracted subduing the prisoners.

Scarlet scrambled into the front passenger seat. Laurel made for the driver's side as Key dove into the back of the van with the women and yanked the door shut behind them.

Robyn stood frozen.

Go or be shot.

Leave behind a few, to save many.

Lose Mom . . . unacceptable.

Laurel, at the edge of the driver's seat, stared helpless at the gearshift and the steering wheel. "Robyn!"

An MP jeep screeched around the corner at the far end of the fence, thumping over the grass toward them.

It was hopeless now. Even if they drove off, they'd be pursued.

"Go," Laurel said to Robyn, her delicate features set in a mask of determination. "Save them." Then she jumped down from the driver's door and set off running—straight toward the oncoming jeep. Robyn had no time to react.

Laurel ran without veering course. She was going to be hit.

"No!" Robyn screamed.

Laurel launched herself like a tiny missile, straight at the jeep's windshield. She splayed her body like a starfish across the glass, blocking the driver's view. The vehicle swerved and lurched, trying to shake the small girl loose. It slowed.

Scarlet pounded the van's horn with her fist. "Now or never," she said.

Robyn stared across the grass at her mother, held tight in the arms of one MP, but still kicking and flailing, rendering him useless for anything but holding her down. She was too far away to be helped. Not without sacrificing the whole group.

"For Sherwood unite," Mrs. Loxley shouted.

The chorus rang up from everywhere. From the other women in the back of the van and the women wrestling the MPs. From Tucker, from Scarlet, even Laurel's gentle voice on the back of the wind:

"For Sherwood, we fight!"

Robyn hopped behind the wheel and accelerated into the night.

≪CHAPTER THIRTY-EIGHT≫

Defiance

The intercom hissed and Crown's assistant's voice slithered through. "She's here, sir."

Crown punched the appropriate button to respond. "Send her in."

The double doors opened and Merryan walked in. She held her hands behind her back. Her toes pointed toward each other as she stood on the thick-pile carpet. Tears rolled down her cheeks.

"Merryan, dear," said Crown. "What is going on?"

"I thought they were my friends," she wept.

"Well," Crown said. "From now on, your friends must be scanned upon entry." He would no longer take children for fools. The moral of tonight's story: he must implement new stricter rules governing the movements of young citizens, citywide.

"You don't have to worry about it," she said. "I don't have many friends. Now I think—I think they all just wanted to see inside the mansion. They never really liked me."

Crown's chest tightened as a feeling akin to pity struck him there. Not exactly pity. Something sharper.

When he spoke, the words came softer, drained of the original anger. "You are not the first to be fooled by those young ruffians."

"I'm sorry," she whispered. "I thought they really liked me."

"You've learned a tough lesson tonight."

"Yes."

"There are very few people you can count on in the world, Merryan." He turned to the window, clasped his hands behind his back. "The more you let in, the more they can take from you."

"I-I can see that now," Merryan stammered. The girl was forever tripping over her words.

"Fortunately, there was little harm done tonight," Crown said. "Some of our guests escaped, true, but the young hoodlums are in custody." He watched carefully for her response to this news.

Merryan began crying in earnest. "You caught them all?"

All. Not "both." Interesting.

"How many friends did you bring over tonight, Merryan?"

There was a small pause as she pulled a tissue from her sleeve and wiped her nose.

"Two," she said.

"Very well."

"They tricked me." She sniffed. "You must be so disappointed in me. I can tell. I make everything difficult."

"It is a privilege to look after you," he told her. "My brother's child. I want you to have everything, as he would have wanted."

"I miss him," Merryan blurted out. "Do you miss him?" She cried still, little choking tears.

It had been a mistake to mention her father. The emotions swirling in the child already had her on edge.

"In the absence of our loved ones, we go on," Crown said. Then he murmured, mostly to himself, "We go on to greatness, if we can."

"Isn't it hard for you, too?" she asked him. "Do you miss your—"

"We go on," Crown snapped, cutting her off. He didn't want to hear the words she was surely about to utter. "We do not look back. I trust it will not happen again."

When she raised her head, her eyes glistened with something other than tears. Crown recognized it. His brother had worn that expression often enough, when he was alive.

"No, Uncle," she said. "I'm very sorry."

Crown narrowed his eyes. "That will be all."

Merryan ducked her head again. "Good night, Uncle."

She shushed across the carpet and slid out the door. He thought of his brother. The look that had lived in his eyes, almost always.

Defiance.

Robyn drove pell-mell through the streets of Castle District. The horrible decision was already made. No turning back. All she wanted now was to put space between them and the MPs.

"Slow down," Key pounded on the cab wall, shouting through the thin metal. "We're pinballing it back here."

Scarlet slammed her hands against the dashboard as Robyn pumped the brakes.

"Buckle up," Robyn said. "If they're following us, we might have to gun it again."

Scarlet leaned over and clipped Robyn's seat belt in place. Robyn didn't dare let go of the wheel at this speed. "Thanks."

Then she scrambled to secure her own seat belt as Robyn took a sharp curve onto a main thoroughfare.

"This is the wrong way," Scarlet told her. "We need to go east."

"We can't go back over the border. No chance."

"We still have the border pass," Scarlet reminded her, pointing to the glove compartment.

"You guys got lucky once." She glanced in the rearview mirror for MP jeeps. "You think it can happen again?"

Scarlet was thoughtful. "No. They know we'll be trying to get back to Sherwood. The border guards will be on high alert."

Robyn slowed the van further, bringing it under the posted traffic limit. If they weren't actively being chased, it was best to try to blend in. "Where are we going to take them?"

"I don't know," Scarlet answered. "We can't keep driving around all night."

"We might have to, until we figure something out."

Scarlet glanced at the van's energy gauge. Three-quarters full.

"Let's try to find a place to park," Robyn said.

"Like where? It's not like we know our way around Castle." Scarlet pounded the door handle. "Dang it. This should've been part of our back-up plan."

Robyn shook her head. "Don't worry." She did know her way around Castle. She knew, for example, how to get home to Loxley Manor from here. Except the MPs had taken over her house.

"We need a store that's open twenty-four hours," Robyn mused out loud. "Somewhere we can park while we figure it out." Yes. She carefully steered into the far lane. They could go to the mall.

Trills of excitement flooded her. A solution! Then she laughed. And laughed. Her hands gripped the wheel and she bent forward, unable to stop.

"What?" Scarlet glanced over, as if concerned that Robyn might be losing it.

"I know where we can go," Robyn answered, between gasps. "I've just—never—gotten this excited—about going—to the mall before." In her old life, she had never understood other girls' fascination with shopping.

Scarlet giggled. A small bursting sound. She tried to hold it back, but she couldn't. "We can, like, totally hang out," she blurted. Soon they were both cracking up.

"What's so funny?" Key shouted. "Get us out of here!"

But to stop the laughter meant silence. Silence meant thoughts, which meant remembering what had happened. So they laughed until their eyes stung.

The TexTer vibrated.

"Sheesh. Does he think we didn't hear him?" Scarlet unclipped the TexTer from her waist. Robyn hadn't been able to take the device onto the Iron Teen course, so Scarlet had held it for her.

"What's he saying?" Robyn asked.

"'Two twenty-seven Shear Line Drive,'" Scarlet read out. "It's an address. 'Safe there,' he says."

It wasn't Key. It had to be the formerly anonymous Bill Pillsbury.

$$\ggg\longrightarrow$$

"She was after the prize money, we believe," Sheriff Mallet told the governor. *Plausible deniability.* "She infiltrated the Iron Teen competition."

"How?" Nick Shiffley leaned his forearms against the back of a chair. "That sounds—"

"Most of the prisoners escaped," Crown thundered, overruling any response. "This is unacceptable."

"If it had happened in my jurisdiction, I'd investigate every MP on duty, and examine every possible crevice in our security," Mallet said firmly. She hoped the reminder that the prison break had happened far from her watch would carry weight. She felt doubly, triply glad that she had played things with the hoodlum so close to the vest. Crown had no reason to suspect that she had once again allowed the girl to slip through her fingers.

"Investigation is underway," Shiffley said. "I recommend you do the same in your jurisdiction." He added snidely, "The hoodlum should never have been able to set foot in this building, much less brought in on a red carpet by our own MPs."

Mallet had one ace left up her sleeve. No choice now but to play it. "Thanks to this contest and the

Sherwood MPs, we have the best lead so far on Robyn Hoodlum."

Shiffley grunted. Crown folded his hands, waiting.

"It's impossible to fake a Tag," Mallet lied. "We now have her true identity. Robyn's name is Roberta Calzone."

The ornate mailbox read Pillsbury. The large house and yard was walled and the driveway gated, similar to Loxley Manor, but the pedestrian gate stood open. Robyn pulled to the curb and slid the gearshift into park.

"Well," Scarlet said. "We don't have any better option. Think we can trust him?"

If you are to succeed in this journey, you will be required to trust. The words of the wise woman, Eveline, floated back to Robyn. "Yes," she said. "He's helped us before."

Scarlet pounded on the back wall. "Let them out," she called to Key.

Robyn preceded the prisoners through the gate and up to the house. An elder woman appeared without so much as a knock, and she motioned the newly freed women inside. They settled onto the sitting room couches, chairs, and rugs. They wept and sighed with relief.

"We can't stay," Robyn said, lingering at the door. "We have to lose the van. It can't be traced to you."

"I'll take care of them," Mrs. Pillsbury said. She was a much older woman, more likely to be Bill Pillsbury's mother than his wife. Maybe he didn't even live here.

"We'll figure out a way to get them to Sherwood," Robyn promised.

"Honey, we can take care of it. Your work is done. Go rest." Mrs. Pillsbury smoothed back the curls alongside Robyn's face. Gently. Like her own mother might do. For a sliver of a second Robyn allowed herself to pretend . . .

She pushed the woman's hands away. "Why are you doing this? Don't you know it's dangerous?"

"All over the city, you will find there are people willing to help you," Mrs. Pillsbury said. "All you have to do is ask."

≪CHAPTER THIRTY-NINE≫

Someone's Child

Robyn, Scarlet, and Key ditched the van in a drugstore parking lot close to Loxley Manor. They began the long, dark walk through the woods back to Sherwood. It wouldn't be as easy to pop out on the other side as it used to be, now that the woods were being heavily patrolled by MPs along the Sherwood side.

But they would cross that bridge when they came to it. Tonight, they needed safety and a chance to regroup. Robyn gasped with relief at the sight of the familiar vine column concealing the spiral stairs.

The tree house was familiar and quiet. The three friends lit a lantern and then lay on the wood planks, depleted. The walk had been long. It was already halfway to morning. There were modest canned goods on the shelves. They should eat. But at first they didn't move.

"I abandoned her," Robyn wept. "We abandoned all of them."

"We didn't have a choice," Key said.

"We're a team," she cried. "We never leave each other behind."

"Sometimes we make sacrifices for the greater good," Scarlet whispered. "They all knew that." She sat against the wall, her knees pulled up to her chest. She looked small, almost as small as Laurel.

Laurel.

Robyn's tears refreshed. "Laurel could have been thrown from the jeep. She could have been killed."

"She's tough," Key said. "I bet she went down swinging."

"She saved us," Scarlet murmured. "I don't know if I would be that brave."

The scene played over and over in Robyn's mind. "Mom threw herself at that guard."

"They all did." Key's voice was alive with wonder. "It was amazing."

"It should be me in prison," Robyn insisted. "I should have found a way to free everyone."

The sheriff had given her a chance to erase everything. She would be in prison now, but her friends might have gotten away with the mansion breakout. They would be okay. Safe. Never to worry again about being part of Robyn Hoodlum's mess. Why hadn't she taken the deal? She hadn't even seriously considered it. She had been too proud, too sure that things could work out, the way they always had before.

Tucker. Laurel. Mom. Robyn was heartbroken with worry. Nothing had gone as planned. Her best effort had made everything worse.

"It should have been me," she repeated.

"Nonsense, girlie," said a gruff voice from the doorway. "We need you free."

The Castle District MPs might not have been the brightest bulbs in the box, but they were able to accurately tell Shiffley what had happened at the fence.

"What did she say next, exactly?" He had homed in on one telling moment of their story.

"'Mom.' She called out for her mother."

"'Mom,'" Shiffley murmured. "In front of a group of female prisoners?"

The MP rustled his boots. "Well, she's a child, you know."

Shiffley glared. As if he needed to be reminded.

Then he spoke. "She's not just a child. She's *someone's* child." He tapped his lip with his thumb. "Bring me a list of those rebel prisoners."

Chazz's lanky frame made the tree house seem much smaller. He folded himself through the doorway. His joints popped and ticked as he settled onto the floor.

"Not sure which is creakier, these old bones or this old shack." He patted the tree-house wall.

"What are you doing here?" Robyn demanded. "How did you find us?"

She wasn't sure what to make of Chazz's responding expression. It read like . . . a smile.

"You ain't that mysterious, girlie." He laughed. "Well, maybe to the authorities, but not to me." His face grew serious. "I come in to tell ya, Jeb's on patrol in another coupla hours. We can walk you outta here then."

"People have heard what happened?"

Chazz nodded. "Some. They's keeping the news tight up, though."

"Jeb will know what happened to the others," Scarlet said. "We can find out."

"Word is, they've moved them," Chazz reported.

"The prisoners?"

"They're no longer being held in the governor's mansion." Chazz looked dismayed to have to continue.

Scarlet leaned forward. "What is it?"

"They've been moved to a camp. Somewhere in Block Six, as far as I can tell."

"The industrial area?" Key sounded troubled.

Chazz confirmed with a nod. "Some kinda work camp."

"Can we break them out?" Robyn said.

"Not likely." Chazz grunted. "Not without some kind of army."

"We'll build an army," she whispered. "If that is what it takes." There were people all over, ready to help. She glanced at Chazz. Perhaps even more than she could imagine.

"When are you going to get it?" Key burst out. "You can't save them. You have to move on."

"We have to save them," Robyn insisted. There was nothing more to say.

"Is this what your parents would've wanted?" Key said. "Stupid risks for selfish reasons?"

"Not just her parents," Scarlet reminded him. "Other political prisoners, too." It still surprised Robyn that Scarlet was the one on her side in all of this. She had been, more often than expected.

Key ignored her, directing his anger at Robyn. "We lost friends last night because you want everything your way."

"You can't have it both ways," Robyn argued. "If I'm supposed to be the one, the leader—then we *should* do it how I want!"

"Like I been telling you," Chazz said to Key. "It'll happen when she's ready."

Robyn's mind closed around that. "Like you've been telling him?" she glared at Key. "Behind my back?"

Chazz coughed. "We got a rebellion to build, girlie. We ain't got time to wait for you to get your act together. Maybe you're the one, maybe you ain't. People still need our help."

So the rebellion wasn't forming anew. It was simmering, all this time, waiting. Her parents, Pillsbury, Chazz, Nessa Croft, and even Key. All working, letting her spin her wheels as if everything was normal. She jumped to her feet. "You lied to me."

"You're going to lose all of us if you keep this up. Then you'll really know what it means to be alone."

≪CHAPTER FORTY≫

The Fire

Robyn ran away from her friends, down the tree-house stairs. In her haste, she stumbled near the bottom of the spiral. She tripped and spun, then fell, landing flat on her back on the floor of the woods. Vines drifted in and out above her, disturbed by the wind of her tumbling body.

Dizzy, she stared upward, catching her breath.

Strange.

The bottom of the tree house wasn't wood. It was stone. She blinked and the vines moved, brushing her skin and stirring her into motion. She jumped up and kept running.

She ran straight out of the woods. She didn't stop to look for patrols. She got lucky.

Luck. Why now? she wondered. *Why not last night?*

Tears streamed down her face. There was no one she could trust. No one to count on. She was alone.

Again. For a minute it had seemed like things were going to be different. Like she had real friends and a shared purpose. But she should have learned her lesson by now.

Robyn's boots pounded the asphalt. She skirted the perimeter of T.C. and—where could she even go?

Back to the cathedral? Without her pendant, she couldn't even go down into the moon shrine.

She stumbled through the stone pillars of the fairground, tears of frustration blinding her. A pair of work-rough hands reached out and pulled her down behind the wall. Robyn gasped and stumbled, too surprised to even cry out.

She came up on her knees, facing Floyd Bridger's stern visage. "You crazy?" he said. "They're patrolling."

"I don't care," Robyn blurted out. "They catch me, I escape." She swiped at her cheeks. "Maybe if I just act ordinary, they'll leave me alone for once."

"You're not an ordinary girl. You're exceptional."

"Stop it." Robyn pressed her hands against her ears, like a small child. As if not hearing it would make it less true.

"I spoke to Chazz," he said. "You're the Loxley girl. It really is you."

The fire. That's what she needed. To see the eternal fire. To look in its flames and try to see in them the mirror she was supposed to see. Her own fire.

Something burned inside her, but it wasn't a righteous feeling. Her chest ached from sobs. From exhaustion. From loneliness.

"I never wanted to be exceptional," she whispered. "I've always been 'exceptional.' You know what that means? It means you're an exception. There's a rule, and you don't fit into it. Everyone else has friends, and you're the exception. Everyone else understands the world and how they fit into it, and you're the exception."

"That's not—"

"Being exceptional sucks," Robyn cried. "I just want to be normal. I just want to"—she choked through the words—"go home."

"The home you want to go back to," Bridger said. "Does it exist anymore?"

What was home now? The cathedral. Being with her friends. Laurel. Key. Tucker. Scarlet. Even Jeb. The people who made her real home felt so far out of reach. Her parents.

"Here," Bridger said. He held out his arms. Another piece of silver cloth draped over them. "Take this."

"More of the curtain?" Robyn sighed. There were no answers in this quest, it seemed. Each supposed revelation brought nothing but problems and questions and puzzles. Bigger and bigger they seemed.

"There is not just one curtain," Bridger told her. "The new pieces belong to the others."

"You told me that," Robyn recalled.

Bridger nodded. "Three shrines, including the one you've already found. The elders know there is little hope of finding—"

"The map was not destroyed," Robyn whispered. The tree house was prominent on the map. The rock fragments at the base of the tree, perhaps they meant something.

Bridger's eyes widened. "You know this for sure?"

"Yes."

He fingered the silky curtain and sighed. "I've never found much comfort in the moon lore texts," he admitted. "It's strange, then, that I've spent so much of my life hunting them."

"Why?"

"Like you, I'm looking for home. In all the wrong places."

"But—"

He handed her the cloth. "This wasn't for me. It wasn't ever for me. I'm one small piece of something bigger. And so are you."

The fire raged in its stone ring at the heart of the tent city. It was otherwise quiet among the cardboard shelters, apart from the muffled murmur of private conversations, and the low hum of blues from a distant radio.

"No more stupid risks," Robyn vowed. "From now on, I'll be in it for the team."

Mallet had taken her pendant. It was a sign. Time to let go of the idea of rescuing her parents. They would want her to move on.

She knew for sure now—her mom would sacrifice herself to push the rebellion forward. To save others. Her parents had been part of something bigger. Something she could carry on.

Robyn pushed back from the fire reluctantly. The heat faded as she stepped away, though she tried to hold it close and carry it with her.

It would be hard to walk back into the cathedral and convince her friends that, finally, she was ready to do the harder thing.

She ran her fingers through her shorn hair as she walked. It would grow back soon enough. Her personal emblem of the moon lore hadn't been destroyed, just temporarily misplaced.

She grinned. Tomorrow would be a whole new day.

Static interrupted the morning bustle of traffic and people noise. Then Crown's voice echoed from the speakers mounted high on the pillars. An announcement, spread citywide.

"This is a message to the hoodlum known as Robyn. We know who you are. We know what you were looking for when you came by tonight. Turn yourself in, or it will be destroyed."

It? Robyn raged against the pronoun. You mean *them*.

Her slip at the mansion was coming back to haunt her. Crown was onto her for sure now. He was threatening Mom and Dad.

A few days ago, this announcement might have sent Robyn into a tailspin. Today, she was stronger. Today, she knew she was not alone.

Robyn picked up her pace. Her crew was waiting. The Crescent Rebellion would have something to say about Crown's threats once and for all.

Today, this news was fuel for the fire.

Acknowledgments

Many people helped in the process of taking this story from idea to reality. Thanks as always to my family for their constant support. I'm grateful for the dear friends and fellow writers who discuss ideas with me, help think through story challenges, listen when the work gets difficult, and celebrate in moments of joy. Special shout-outs to Nicole, who finds the good in everything; Will, Alice, Liam, and Iris, who are always willing to feed me dinner when I'm on deadline; Emily, who reminds me it's okay to be me; Sarah, who has become my sister; and Peter, who helps Robyn more than he knows. I cherish my colleagues at Vermont College of Fine Arts, for the knowledge and sense of community they offer me. Thanks to Michelle Humphrey. Most of all, thanks to my editor, Mary Kate Castellani, along with Brett

Wright, Courtney Griffin, Beth Eller, Linette Kim, and everyone at Bloomsbury who works to help get Robyn's stories onto the page and out into the world.

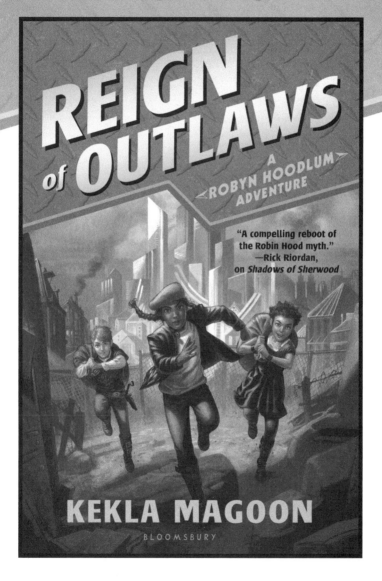

The cathedral fell quiet. Everyone waited for Robyn to speak. Everyone included Key, Scarlet, Chazz, Nessa Croft, Floyd Bridger, and two men and six women Robyn didn't recognize.

In the great arching space of the cathedral, the group seemed small, even though more people had arrived than she expected.

"I don't know everyone here," Robyn said.

The adults introduced themselves. One woman spoke, "We are the remaining few who started this Crescendo and have not yet been imprisoned."

The "yet" echoed through the air, seeming to bounce off every pillar and arch.

Another said, "Together we all represent the past, present, and future of the Crescent Rebellion. Watching you these past few months, I feel renewed hope."

"Then why did you lie to me?" Robyn couldn't help the question.

"You can't see what you're not ready for," Chazz said. "You know there was a movement. Why weren't you looking to see what had gone before?"

"I thought all the leaders were imprisoned. I saw Nyna Campbell tied up on that stage. I saw the wanted posters for Nessa and Bridger." Robyn nodded to him. "I saw it all the day we first met. I thought we were alone in seeing what needed to be done."

"You came to see me in T.C."

"And you tried to send me packing," she accused Chazz. "You told me flat out to run, that it was useless to stay and fight."

Chazz gazed back at her, seemingly emotionless.

"Now Crown's threatening my parents. I think he's figured out who I am."

Chazz reacted to that. "Then let's focus on the problem at hand. How do we get them out?"

"What did Crown really say?" Key argued. "He didn't mention your parents specifically. He didn't even say 'they.' He said 'it.'"

Robyn recited the message for those who had not heard it firsthand.

"That's vague. He might have been bluffing," Scarlet agreed.

"He could be trying to trick you into turning yourself in," Key said.

No. Robyn knew she had screwed up. She'd called out "Mom" when the guards had grabbed her mother. It would be very easy to put those pieces together. Even for the most thick-headed MPs. With her parents still in Crown's custody, she couldn't take the chance.

"I don't think he's bluffing," Robyn said. She pulled a long slow breath into her lungs. She knew what came next, but it was the hardest thing she'd ever had to utter.

"My parents would want the rebellion to continue," Robyn said. "With or without them." It was especially hard to choke out the last bit. For months now, her sole goal had been to save them. The knot in her chest refused to go away.

But things were different now.

She had watched her mother sacrifice herself for the cause. Robyn understood now what her purpose was. What it all meant.

Robyn's limbs felt heavy. She stood rooted to the spot on the altar. Finally, she forced the weightiest thoughts into words.

"In seventy-two hours, my parents will be killed. We can't stage a rescue in that short a time. But we can send Crown a message."

"What kind of message?" Scarlet asked.

"The message that we are not scared. That this rebellion cannot be crushed by his threats." Robyn paced along the altar. "He knows who I am. He thinks all I